MW01615621

NOWHERE LEFT.

(A Harley Cole FBI Suspense Thriller—Book 2)

Kate Bold

Kate Bold

Bestselling author Kate Bold is author of the ALEXA CHASE SUSPENSE THRILLER series, comprising six books (and counting); the ASHLEY HOPE SUSPENSE THRILLER series, comprising six books (and counting); the CAMILLE GRACE FBI SUSPENSE THRILLER series, comprising five books (and counting); and the HARLEY COLE FBI SUSPENSE THRILLER series, comprising three books (and counting).

An avid reader and lifelong fan of the mystery and thriller genres, Kate loves to hear from you, so please feel free to visit www.kateboldauthor.com to learn more and stay in touch.

Copyright © 2022 by Kate Bold. All rights reserved. Except as permitted under the U.S. Copyright Act of 1976, no part of this publication may be reproduced, distributed or transmitted in any form or by any means, or stored in a database or retrieval system, without the prior permission of the author. This ebook is licensed for your personal enjoyment only. This ebook may not be re-sold or given away to other people. If you would like to share this book with another person, please purchase an additional copy for each recipient. If you're reading this book and did not purchase it, or it was not purchased for your use only, then please return it and purchase your own copy. Thank you for respecting the hard work of this author. This is a work of fiction. Names, characters, businesses, organizations, places, events, and incidents either are the product of the author's imagination or are used fictionally. Any resemblance to actual persons, living or dead, is entirely coincidental. Jacket image Copyright Galyna Andrushko, used under license from Shutterstock.com.
ISBN: 978-1-0943-3000-6

BOOKS BY KATE BOLD

ALEXA CHASE SUSPENSE THRILLER
THE KILLING GAME (Book #1)
THE KILLING TIDE (Book #2)
THE KILLING HOUR (Book #3)
THE KILLING POINT (Book #4)
THE KILLING FOG (Book #5)
THE KILLING PLACE (Book #6)

ASHLEY HOPE SUSPENSE THRILLER
LET ME GO (Book #1)
LET ME OUT (Book #2)
LET ME LIVE (Book #3)
LET ME BREATHE (Book #4)
LET ME FORGET (Book #5)
LET ME ESCAPE (Book #6)

CAMILLE GRACE FBI SUSPENSE THRILLER
NOT ME (Book #1)
NOT NOW (Book #2)
NOT WELL (Book #3)
NOT HER (Book #4)
NOT NORMAL (Book #5)

HARLEY COLE FBI SUSPENSE THRILLER
NOWHERE SAFE (Book #1)
NOWHERE LEFT (Book #2)
NOWHERE TO RUN (Book #3)

PROLOGUE

Isla leaned against the tree, sucking in gulps of dry desert air as she tried to catch her breath. She twisted her neck to stare up the slope behind her, searching for any movement against the starry skyline. She saw nothing but boulders, creosote bushes, and the occasional juniper tree, the same kind that she was leaning against now.

Maybe he went back, she thought, trying to gather enough saliva to swallow. Her mouth was as sticky as a tar pit. Sweat ran freely down her cheeks, and she knuckled it away from her eyes as she studied the shadows.

It didn't make sense. She had been returning with a bundle of firewood in her arms when, as she neared the house, a figure stepped out from the protective screen of a mesquite and made a clumsy grab at her. On instinct, she threw the bundle of sticks at her attacker before fleeing.

Not, however, before glimpsing the dark hollows of the stranger's eyes, glinting with rabid intensity beneath the shade of his brow.

Now, pausing on the wooded slope, she tried to imagine who would want to harm her. Did someone have a grudge against her because she and Joseph were in love? He had no shortage of admirers in the community. One of the other girls, perhaps?

No. Much as they might have hated her, Isla didn't think they had the guts to pull a stunt like this. Besides, they were too small. This person had been larger, more like…

A shudder passed through her.

No, she told herself. *Joseph would never harm you. He was the one who invited you to the community, after all. Besides, he promised you'll be together forever.*

She might be only fifteen and he forty-two, but what did age matter when it came to love? Their love was true, their love was *real*, and it didn't matter how many times her strung-out mother told her she belonged with a boy her age. She had seen what boys her age did, oh yes. They brought you behind the bleachers, and then they *took* you.

Yes, that was what it was: taking. Cutting you open, pulling out something you didn't know you had in there, and consuming it right in

1

front of you. Then leaving you like a crumpled pack of cigarettes at the side of the road.

Joseph would never treat her that way. He loved her, admired her. He spoke beautiful things to her in French that she didn't understand, but she knew they were lovely because of how he said them. He saw the other girls sometimes, too, and this knowledge always sent a stab of pain right through Isla's heart, but he assured her he was only nurturing them, like a gardener tending his plants. It was a sign of their neediness, not their worthiness. She, Isla, was his one and only.

And soon he was going to prove it by going away with her— forever. He had promised her that very thing just last night, and Joseph was not a man to break his promises.

Isla's thoughts were broken by the clicking of a pebble as it came tumbling down the slope. A shadow detached itself from behind a boulder and began to ooze down toward Isla, soundless in the night air.

A bright burst of panic went off in Isla's mind. She rushed down through the trees, her skinny legs trembling with the effort of slowing her descent. Fatigue built up like lead in her muscles until finally she stepped on a stone and her ankle rolled beneath her. She heard a popping sound as her full weight – not much over a hundred pounds, but still enough – came down on the ankle.

Crying aloud, she fell headlong across the stony ground and rolled to her back, panting. Throbs of pain came up from her ankle in waves. She lifted her leg and, to her horror, saw her foot dangling from it, unsupported.

Get up, get up! the voice of fear screamed in her mind. Another part of her mind, however, told her to stay down and play dead.

All she had to do was wait. Then, when she was alone again, she would hobble back up the slope and knock on Joseph's window, and he would look after her. He would know what to do.

She closed her eyes, clamping down on the pain. When she opened them again, she saw an inky shadow leaning over her, blotting the stars. She could just make out a sketch of the face.

And to her terror, she recognized it.

Impossible, she thought.

She screamed. The sound cut through the trees and rolled across the slopes of the mountains.

No echo returned, however, but a cold, dry laugh.

CHAPTER ONE

Harley Cole turned the volume up on the stereo as she listened to the voicemail recording, her trained eyes scanning the desert with an unconscious vigilance that was the product of her eleven years with the Bureau. The U-Haul behind her, packed with all the worldly possessions worth taking back with her from Massachusetts (mostly criminology textbooks, clothes, and a few pieces of furniture she couldn't bear to part with), bumped and jounced along the dirt road, kicking up a wake of dust.

"It's about Kelly," came the weathered voice of Luis Santiago, the sheriff of Huerta County, where Harley had been born and raised. He also happened to have served as deputy during the investigation into Kelly's disappearance.

"There's been a development," he added.

Even though Harley had already listened to the message several times in the past few weeks while finalizing the divorce with Rob and planning her move to New Mexico, even though Kelly had been missing for seventeen years and Harley had realized long ago that there was a good chance she would never learn why Kelly had vanished from her tent in the middle of the night during a camping trip with friends, the mention of her sister's name still sent a thrill through her body.

Was it fear that this might confirm the obvious? Or was it a residual hope that maybe, just maybe, there was a tiny piece of evidence to suggest Kelly *hadn't* been dead all these years?

"I debated whether or not to say anything," the sheriff continued in a cautious voice that suggested he was trying to help manage Harley's expectations. "Seems a cruel thing, getting your hopes up for nothing. But I promised I'd share anything I found."

He paused, as if unsure how much to say over the phone.

"I know you've already flown back home," he continued, "but if you can call me back, I'd love to discuss this in more detail with you."

The voicemail ended, leaving Harley to wonder just what the sheriff had discovered and how significant it could be. With a case this old, the chance of turning over something new was incredibly unlikely. Still, a man like Luis Santiago didn't reach out just to shoot the breeze. If he had something to say, Harley was ready to listen.

3

All she had to do was drop off her things at the new house she was renting, then swing by his office, and they could sit down for a long chat. It was a Friday, and she wasn't scheduled to report to the Santa Fe field office until Monday, so she had time.

Harley was still thinking about the voicemail as she crested a hill and saw a row of traffic cones strung out across the road. A sign reading ROAD CLOSED stood on the yellow lines, its feet held down by sandbags. Police cars and a pair of ambulances were parked farther down the road, along with a two-toned Ford pickup that looked like it had a decade on Harley.

Harley slowed, her gaze shifting to the knot of figures gathered at the side of the road, close to the ambulances. Most of them wore the charcoal-black uniforms of local PD, but Harley noticed an undyed Stetson standing a head taller than the rest. The head swiveled, lips pressed together in a thoughtful frown as the eyes – hidden behind a pair of aviator sunglasses – studied Harley's vehicle. He said something to the group of officers before detaching himself and moving toward Harley with long, slow strides.

Harley stepped out of the vehicle and felt the heat of the sunbaked asphalt begin wicking up through her tennis shoes. Vultures circled in the distance beneath tatters of cloud.

The man stopped a few feet away and planted his hands on his hips. "You just couldn't stay away, could you?" he said.

She shaded her eyes against the sunlight. "What can I say? I'm a glutton for punishment."

The man held that hard stare a few moments longer. Then his face broke into an easy grin as he stuck out his hand. "Wasn't sure I'd ever see you again," he said as they shook. "This mean you took the job?"

"Looks like it."

Harley studied the face of Anthony Callaway, who had been her partner on the Felix Navarro case just a few weeks earlier. They had learned to work well together, despite their differences. After the conclusion of the case, she had gone back east fully expecting to pick up the pieces of her life there. The offer of a job working out of the Santa Fe office, however, had proved too strong—not to mention Sheriff Santiago's hint about Kelly.

"Well," Callaway said, adjusting his Stetson, "for what it's worth, I'm glad you took the job. We can never have enough good agents."

"I'm looking forward to being more than just a consultant," Harley answered. "It makes you feel naked, walking around without that badge."

Callaway nodded thoughtfully. "This doesn't mean I have to start treating you like an equal, though, does it?"

"Oh, no. That would be ridiculous."

There was a beat of uncertain silence. Though it was good to see Callaway again, Harley was not entirely sure how to pick up where they'd left off. She could talk for hours about a case, but when it came to chit-chat, she sometimes struggled to find her direction. It was part of the reason she didn't have many friends outside the Bureau.

"Listen," she said, "I'd better get going. I have a lot of unpacking to do this weekend."

Callaway looked surprised. "What, are you kidding? You're already at a crime scene, and you're going to walk away without even seeing the body?"

Harley felt that old, familiar curiosity stirring within her, the same curiosity she had felt in the weeks and months following her sister's disappearance. Back then she had fed her curiosity with newspaper articles, crime books, and interviews she had recorded in her little spiral notebook. Now, however, she had access to the real thing: hard evidence. And the truth could be addicting.

A knowing smile pulled at Callaway's mouth. "Come on, just take a look. Maybe you'll pick up on something I missed. Besides, you have all weekend to unpack."

Before Harley could protest, Callaway was shouting to a nearby officer. "Hey, Bodie!"

The officer turned, hands resting on his belt. He gave a sharp, upward nod to show he was listening.

"Keep an eye on the U-Haul? My partner and I are going to take another look at the body."

Partner, Harley mused as Bodie shuffled toward the vehicle. She thought of the cold way Callaway had treated her the first time they'd met. A lot had happened since then, however. There was nothing like saving one another's lives to engender mutual respect.

"Can't say this was the welcome I was expecting," she said as she followed Callaway down the road. "I was planning to be a civilian until Monday."

Callaway grunted his amusement. "And miss all the fun?"

CHAPTER TWO

Harley felt her pulse quickening in anticipation as she followed Callaway down the road. As reluctant as she was to admit it, crime was as much a drug to her as it was to many criminals. It felt good to hit the ground running, even though she had too much to do at her new place to help with the investigation.

"Local PD is under-staffed," Callaway explained. "Budget cuts, bureaucratic bullshit, you know how it goes. We just wrapped up a sexual assault case, so Newbury thought it would be a sign of goodwill to send me down here to lend a hand."

Harley nodded, studying the area. The desert on either side was peppered with juniper bushes and scraggly grasses, rising toward a tumble of hills that dominated the horizon. A raven perched on the shriveled remains of a coyote, glancing up to give a sharp "Caw!" at the visitors before taking flight.

As they neared the scene of the crime, Harley watched a woman in a plastic white suit and mint green gloves lean into her tripod-mounted camera to take a snapshot of the body. Numbered yellow cards were staggered about the area, marking evidence.

The victim lay sprawled on her back in the withered grass fringing the road, arms stretched over her head like a diver jumping into a pool. A mop of curly black hair hid most of her face, leaving only a protruding chin, childlike in its roundness. Ugly purple-yellow bruises colored her throat. Two rows of faint tire tracks could be seen in the flattened grass.

Harley studied the brittle elasticity of the victim's tanned skin. "What do you think? Mid-forties?"

"Mid-to-late," Callaway agreed, handing Harley a pair of plastic gloves before putting on his own. "No ID. We're running her prints, so we'll see if we get any hits."

His voice was professional, all hint of levity gone. It was impressive to Harley how easily Callaway could switch hats. She wondered if it took a toll on him, this line of work. She'd like to think it hadn't taken a toll on her, but the fate of her former marriage suggested otherwise.

"Strangulation?" she said.

Callaway nodded. "Looks that way. In this heat, she can't have been out here long. An hour, maybe, two at the most."

Harley squatted down to examine the woman's outstretched right arm. A sleeve of tattoos covered elbow to wrist, all vines and flowers.

"Nature-lover, by the look of it," Callaway observed.

Harley nodded. The clothes – a plain white dress with pink flowers – struck her as odd. There was something unusual about the tailoring, but she wasn't sure what.

"Look how stiff her arms are," Harley murmured. "He must have stretched her out, probably as he was dragging her body into a vehicle. Then rigor mortis set in."

"He? You're assuming it's a man?"

"Ninety percent of homicides are perpetrated by men," Harley answered. "Besides, it's a little confusing to say 'they' when we're probably talking about only one person."

Callaway raised an eyebrow. "Again, seems like an assumption. It could have been two men—or two women, for that matter. A whole mob of people, maybe."

Harley shook her head. "No, my money's on one killer. This whole situation has panic written all over it. He kills the woman, then gets rid of the body. But he doesn't bury it. Why not?"

"Maybe he wasn't hiding the body. Maybe he put it here for us to find it, like a trophy."

"Then leave her on the highway, in the city—somewhere obvious. This is too…" She paused, searching for the word. "Remote. Maybe he wasn't the only one involved in the crime, but I'll bet he was the only one involved in getting rid of the body. I don't think he had a plan for what to do, or if he did, he got sidetracked. This looks like a Plan B to me, not a Plan A."

It felt good, the way the thoughts hummed through her mind like high-speed traffic. She had missed this in the past few weeks, like a bodybuilder who goes without lifting weights for a time due to injury. The speed at which the details locked together in her mind only confirmed what she already knew: She was good at this.

"Okay," Callaway said patiently, playing along. "So let's assume for a minute you're correct and we're dealing with one killer, a man. How does he get her body out here? A trunk?"

"Pickup," Harley answered without hesitation.

Callaway sighed, rubbing his forehead. "You're gonna tell me you can read that from the tire tracks?"

"Not the tire tracks." She pointed to a small brown object clinging to the underside of the victim's clothes. "That."

Callaway stooped to examine it closely. "Bark?"

Harley nodded. "Bits of leaves in her hair, too."

"But only the back," Callaway said, catching on. "You think the killer puts her in the back of a pickup, drives her out here, then…" He mimed grabbing a pair of ankles at waist-height and pulling.

"It would explain the debris beneath her," she answered.

"Seems risky. What if someone spotted the body while the killer was transporting her here?"

She paused. "The sun rises at, what, six? And it's…" She reached for her phone, but Callaway read his watch before she could reach it.

"Ten-o-eight," he said. "If he dropped her off in the last hour or two, it would have been broad daylight."

"Then he must have covered her."

She leaned over the victim's wrists, searching for burns or any other signs of restraints. She noticed a series of faint white scars on the underside of the right wrist.

"Looks like she was a cutter," Harley observed. "The scars are old."

She straightened, not sure what to do with this new piece of evidence. "Has forensics checked beneath the nails?" she said. "I don't see any indication of restraints, so there's a good chance she fought back."

"They took samples," he answered. "Cast the tire tracks, too, though there's not much to go on, given all the grass."

Harley bit her lower lip. She was still thinking about how the killer had transported the body. As she circled the victim, she noticed an earring hidden beneath the halo of curly hair. It appeared to be leather cut in the shape of a leaf. A thin blue strand was caught on the metal.

Harley pulled out her phone and took three pictures of the strand, just to be sure. Then, using one hand to carefully brush the victim's hair aside, she pulled the strand free. Callaway passed her an evidence bag, and she slipped the thread inside.

"What does that look like to you?" she said, holding it up.

"A tarp," Callaway mused. Neither spoke for several moments. There was something both chilling and exhilarating about putting together the pieces of a crime. Harley loved the challenge, yet with every new piece of evidence the crime became a little more real, a little more terrible.

Callaway said, "So you think he puts the body in the back of his truck, covers her with a tarp?"

8

Harley shrugged. "A pickup driving down the road with a tarp in back. Who's going to notice?"

Callaway rubbed his jawline, making a faint rasping sound like sandpaper against wood. "Doesn't narrow down the pool of suspects much, though. Just about everyone around here drives a truck. Different in the cities, sure, but in the country…"

Something else about the body, however, had caught Harley's attention. She stared at it, puzzled.

"Harley?" Callaway said. "Still with us?"

"Her clothes. Anything strike you as odd about them?"

Callaway shrugged. "They're probably not the latest fashion in Paris, but…"

"I wore a dress just like that when I was a kid—got it from a roadside vendor." It was fairly common to see someone at the side of the road selling clothes, firewood, fry bread, corn, or other items from the back of a truck, an old shack, or even an RV. It was something she had missed when she moved east. There was nothing quite like a fresh, hot tamale.

Harley lifted the fabric and began studying the seams. She was no seamstress, but the irregularities in the stitching – not to mention the absence of tags – suggested what she had already suspected.

"This dress was homemade," she mused.

Callaway's face brightened suddenly. "You know, there's a place not too far from here sells that kind of thing." He snapped his fingers. "What's the name of it…"

Looking up, he called to a nearby officer. "Hey, Ned! What's that place where all the people live without electricity or anything?"

"You mean the one with the kids always throwing rocks at cars?"

"That's the one!"

"Holy Hope Community, I think it's called."

Callaway turned back to Harley. "There you go. I'm pretty sure everything they wear is homemade—wouldn't want to support the evil empire that is capitalism." He grunted. "If anyone around here can tell us about homemade clothes, it's them."

Harley nodded. "Sounds like we should check them out."

"We can take my truck. Just give Bodie your address, and he'll make sure your things get to your house, safe and sound."

Harley walked a few paces and then stopped. She had gotten so wrapped up in the details of the case that she had forgotten her weekend plans. Callaway's mention of her address, however, reminded her she didn't have so much as a bed set up at the new place.

"What is it?" Callaway said, studying her.

"It's just that if I go with you, I'm committing to this thing. In for a penny, in for a pound. I don't believe in half measures, not when we're looking for a murderer." She sighed. "It's almost like I can't help myself."

A sunny smile dawned on Callaway's face. "And you're just realizing this now?"

CHAPTER THREE

Harley watched for a mob of stone-throwing children as they followed the winding dirt road up into the hills, but she saw none. She did, however, notice other signs of life: stacks of rocks, like those used to mark hiking trails, hand paintings on walls of sheer stone, rope walkways dangling from trees. It felt to Harley like they were entering a primitive culture reenactment.

"They're skilled hunters, several of them," Callaway observed as he drove. "Bow-and-arrow hunters, mostly. You should see the way they stalk elk."

Staring at a small hole dug into the side of a hill, it occurred to Harley that her father would have loved such a place. He had always been an avid outdoorsman, at least until the lung cancer limited him. He was the reason Harley enjoyed hiking as much as she did—as well as the reason that Kelly had gone on that camping trip so many years ago, a fact that no doubt haunted him from time to time.

I need to make time to see him, she thought. *There's no telling when it'll be the last time.*

They had both made plenty of mistakes in the relationship, but Harley was determined to bury the hatchet and start fresh, even if they didn't have much time left to work with.

As they came around a bend, Harley was distracted from her thoughts by a large wooden sign reading "HOLY HOPE COMMUNITY: ALL ARE WELCOME" in bright, cheerful slashes of paint. Handprints — some the size of Callaway's hands, some as small as those of a raccoon — patterned the wood around the central message in a chaotic tumble of colors.

"I can see the appeal," Harley said. "Your own little community out here, far from the noise and pollution."

"Until you sit on the outhouse seat in the dead of winter," Callaway observed dryly.

The community was situated on a shelf in the wooded hills. To the right, high hills dotted with scrub growth overlooked the community; to the left, the ground fell away toward the distant plains. The most striking characteristic, however, was how green the valley was. Plant life bloomed on every side: clusters of aspen, towering rows of cottonwoods, golden forsythias, and other shrubs Harley could not name.

"There's a subterranean river not far beneath the surface," Callaway said. "Only thing keeping this place alive."

"I might have to take my next vacation here," Harley mused, half-joking and half-serious. Her attention turned from the plants to the rows of adobe houses flanking the road, all with brightly-painted doors and windows. Every yard had a small vegetable garden. In the middle of the community (Harley thought of it as the town square) stood a large fire pit covered by a canopy and surrounded by long wooden benches. Harley guessed it was where the community held group meetings.

As they neared the center of the community, Harley noticed eyes watching them from all sides. An old woman hoeing a garden straightened to stare at them. Beside her, a younger man was clearing weeds with a pitchfork. He paused to look up, wiping sweat from his face with a bandanna as he stared at the vehicle.

"Think they drive automobiles?" Harley mused aloud.

"You didn't see the lot back there?"

Harley shook her head. She had been too distracted to notice.

"They keep maybe four or five vehicles. Most of the time they go on foot or ride bicycles, but a few still like to drive. It's not against the rules, though it is frowned upon to depend on automobiles too much."

"I'm surprised they don't have horses and buggies."

Callaway chuckled. "We're a little far south for Amish country, in case you haven't noticed."

Callaway parked close to the town square. As the two agents got out, a group of dirty-faced children emerged from between a pair of houses, chattering excitedly as they raced toward the vehicle. They pulled up at a cautious distance, their faces going blank as they stared up at the towering Callaway.

Their clothes are so plain, Harley observed. *Not a printed design anywhere.* She couldn't help wondering if their clothes had been handmade just like the victim's, possibly by the same person.

As Harley moved around the hood of the truck to join Callaway, she hoped these kids weren't the rock-throwing variety. She didn't want to go down in history as the first federal agent stoned to death by children.

The children, however, showed nothing but curiosity as Callaway doffed his Stetson and smiled at them. "You kids ever seen an FBI badge before?" he said, unclipping his badge and holding it up for all the children to see the golden eagle gleam in the sunlight. Several of the children reached out grubby hands, begging him to let them hold it.

One of the children, however, a scrawny boy with freckled cheeks and a large gap between his front teeth that gave his words a hollow whistling sound, folded his arms. "You're not supposed to be here," he said.

"Why's that?" Callaway replied, smiling.

"Police don't belong here."

Harley kept her voice friendly. "Good thing we're not police. We're government agents."

The boy muttered something. Harley missed most of it, but she thought she caught the word "pigs." She was about to ask the boy to repeat himself when an older woman joined in.

"That's enough, Roslin," she said. She had long hair, equal parts gray and white, braided down the sides of her head with beads. She set her hand on the boy's head (Harley noticed the crescents of dirt beneath the woman's fingernails), and the boy scurried away as if shocked by an electrical current.

"My name's Melissa Hargrave," the woman said, smiling and placing her hand across her chest. "Around here, though, I'm just called Gardenia."

"Gardenia," Callaway repeated with polite interest. "That's a lovely nickname. I'm Agent Callaway, this is Agent Cole. We're with the FBI."

A shadow passed over Gardenia's face. "It's not often we have federal agents here at Holy Hope—and pardon me for saying so, but I can't imagine it's a good sign you're here, not unless you've come to deliver a few tax refunds in person."

Callaway gave an easygoing chuckle. "Afraid that's not within our purview."

"We're investigating a homicide," Harley said, cutting to the chase. She held up her phone, which displayed a picture of the body they had discovered that morning. "Have you seen this woman before?"

Gardenia recoiled, covering her mouth with a hand spotted brown with age. "I—I don't know. Where did you find her? Is she dead?"

"Take your time," Callaway said gently. "This is very important. We found her body over on Coyote Creek Road just this morning."

Gardenia concentrated on the picture for a few seconds before looking away, her gaze tracking a trio of boys pretending to shoot at one another with sticks. "No, I've never seen her. Or if I have, it's been a very long time."

This response puzzled Harley. She couldn't say for sure whether the woman was lying, but she felt sure she was hiding something. She suspected Gardenia hadn't turned away out of discomfort so much as a desire to hide her feelings.

"Mind if we ask around?" Callaway said. "See if anyone else might have known her?"

Gardenia's eyes flicked back to Callaway. There was a wariness in them now that hadn't been there before. "May I ask what connection you're trying to make here?"

"Her clothing," Harley explained, putting her phone away. "It appears to have been homemade, so we thought she might have got it here."

"Well, that clears things up," Gardenia answered with a little laugh of relief. "We have several skilled seamstresses here—I'm one of them, in fact. We make clothes and sell them at local markets. You should stop by one of those, see if anyone there has seen your victim."

"We'll be sure to do that," Harley answered with a tight smile. "But we'd still like to ask around, since we're already here." She was not going to be dismissed so easily.

That wary look returned to Gardenia's face.

"Just crossing our *t*'s and dotting our *i*'s, you know," Callaway added for reassurance. "Then we'll be on our way."

Gardenia gazed off into the distance. Harley could almost hear the gears shifting in the old woman's mind, though what she was thinking about, Harley could not tell.

Finally she turned back toward the two agents and smiled, all trace of concern gone. "It's a free country, isn't it? You're welcome to talk to anyone—even the squirrels, if you're so inclined. They'll probably have more to say than anyone else."

"Why might that be?" Callaway said.

"We're the first generation here at Holy Hope. Most of our people joined the community to escape pasts of addiction or abuse, or simply to get out of the rat race. I mean no offense when I say that; for some of them, government agents like yourselves represent everything they've worked so hard to get away from."

She smiled, as if to indicate she didn't bear any personal ill-will toward them. Before Harley could think of a follow-up question, a young man with disheveled hair poked his head out from one of the houses and called to her.

"Mother! Freedom is going into labor!"

Gardenia flashed a regretful smile at the agents. "We hold life sacred here," she said quickly. "So if you're looking for a killer, my suggestion is you look elsewhere." With that, she hurried away in a flurry of skirts.

Harley watched the woman disappear inside the house. "Is it just me," she murmured, "or was she doing everything she could to convince us we were wasting our time?"

"Can you blame her?" Callaway answered in a low voice. "They work so hard to separate themselves from society, only to have two federal agents show up searching for a murderer. They might seem a little oddball, but at the end of the day, all they're looking for is some peace and quiet."

"Let's just hope we don't have to drag one of them away in cuffs."

Harley felt like an outsider already, simply because she had spent so many years in the northeast. She had lost touch with the slow pace of life down here, and nowhere was the contrast more striking than in the midst of an off-grid community where there was no such thing as punching a time clock or turning on the evening news. It was going to take some time for her to adjust.

A teenage girl carrying a basket of vegetables walked along the far side of the road. She moved as if she would happily crawl into a hole in the ground at the first opportunity: head hanging forward with her hair hiding her face, shoulders hunched, feet shuffling along the ground.

"Excuse me, miss?" Harley said, crossing toward the girl. "Can you tell me if you recognize this woman?"

The girl looked up, her eyes going wide with fear. Then she hurried forward, ignoring Harley's request. She disappeared inside one of the houses, casting a frightened glance back at the two agents as she closed the door.

"That was odd," Callaway said.

"Maybe her parents taught her not to talk to strangers," Harley suggested. She did not know whether to chalk it up to teenage social anxiety or if there was something more going on.

She was still pondering this when Callaway gestured toward a trio of middle-aged men seated at a table on the far side of the street. "Let's go ask those gentlemen," he said. "They look talkative."

The three men had beards of varying colors: one blonde, one gray, one charcoal black. They were smoking pipes and discussing the views of Albert Camus, an author Harley had read in college but remembered precious little about.

The conversation fell silent as the two agents reached the three men. The faces of the men grew stoic, their eyes flat.

"Sorry to interrupt," Callaway said. "We'd just like a moment of your time. We're looking for—"

Before Callaway could finish, the three men pushed back their chairs, rose, and moved away, splitting off in separate directions. It looked almost like it had been choreographed.

Harley stared after them, baffled by their reaction. "Do you ever feel like a *persona non grata*?"

"More by the second," Callaway answered. "I knew they didn't have a high opinion of law enforcement, but I didn't know it was *this* bad."

Harley set her jaw, undeterred. "Well, we're not going away that easily. We'll go door to door, if we have to."

"Wasting your time," a nearby voice said.

They glanced over to see a long-haired man sitting on a log nearby, whittling a piece of wood. He appeared to be making an ax handle. Long coils of wood flew off the knife and tumbled to the ground, bright against the packed earth.

"What do you mean by that?" Callaway answered, stepping toward him.

"Stay where you are," the man hissed. "Sit down at the table, would you? You want to get me blackballed?"

Callaway raised an eyebrow at Harley.

This place gets stranger by the second, Harley mused.

"I guess we act like we're talking with each other," Harley said in a low voice as she and Callaway sat down across from one another. "We should look around, pretend we're enjoying the sights."

Callaway leaned back, laying his long arms across the table. His hands were large and calloused—a working man's hands. Tiny yellow slivers were buried in the skin around the nails. Hay slivers, she guessed. It was a subtle reminder that Callaway had a life beyond this job, a life Harley knew very little about.

"Can we show you the picture?" Callaway said, staring at Harley but speaking to the whittler.

"Already saw it when you were flashing it around."

"And do you recognize her?" Harley answered.

The man was silent for several moments. The knife made a *hwick, hwick* sound as it shaved the wood.

"Is she dead?" he said.

"Afraid so," Callaway answered. "Did you know her?"

16

Another long silence. Finally he said, "We can't do this here. My house is way down at the end—one with all the rain barrels. On the right. Meet me there in five minutes."

With that he got up, tossed his hair, and disappeared between two of the buildings.

CHAPTER FOUR

Callaway knocked at the door of the adobe hut. As he waited for an answer, he stole a cautious glance at Harley, who was looking away. He had forgotten how much taller he was, probably because the size of her personality more than compensated for the difference. Her back was ramrod-straight, her hair tied neatly behind her head, a tasteful hint of eyeshadow giving her eyes a mysterious touch. A silver chain Callaway hadn't previously noticed hung around her neck.

Callaway hadn't expected Harley to take the job; she didn't seem like the kind of person to retrace her steps. Now that she was here, however, he had mixed feelings. He knew she was a competent field agent – the Navarro case had assured him of that – but he couldn't help wondering about the investigation opened by the Office of Professional Responsibility to examine her pursuit of John Kavers, a serial murderer who Harley had helped put away. She had been put on leave for her efforts, which was why she had come west to visit family—and ended up working as a consultant on the Navarro case.

What had she done? She got results, that much was clear, but at what cost? How much did he need to worry that her tactics might jeopardize this case or any future cases they might work on together?

I'll just have to ask her about it, straight up, he thought. *As soon as we have a chance to talk.*

And in the meantime, he would just have to hope she wouldn't screw things up.

The door opened, and the whittler they had previously spoken with poked his head out. He looked left and right – it seemed almost cartoonish, the way he craned his neck – before darting back inside. Callaway entered a moment later, followed by Harley.

The smell of woodsmoke filled the low, dark room. The floor was bare earth, the furniture – bed, table, a set of four chairs – made of hand-carved wood.

"Sorry for all the secrecy," the man said, poking at the smoldering fire with a broken branch. "Some of the others don't like having visitors from the outside world—feels like an invasion. Hard for the kids to go back to playing with sticks after they've seen a Game Boy, know what I mean?"

Callaway took off his hat, as much to avoid hitting the ceiling as to show respect. "Sure," he answered, recoiling as he bumped into some kind of root hanging from the joists. "You want to protect them."

"And forget talking to the police," the man went on, as if Callaway hadn't spoken. "You're just a reminder we still have to pay taxes for services we don't need."

"I'm sorry to interrupt," Harley said. "I don't think we caught your name." She pulled out her phone, probably so she could take notes.

She really has a way of sticking out like a sore thumb, Callaway thought, and for a brief moment he wondered if it had been a mistake to invite her to see the body back on Coyote Creek Road. Then again, hadn't he shown her the body so she would jump into the case with both feet? They'd made a good team, working the Navarro case together. Who was to say they couldn't be equally successful again?

Still, the OPR investigation…

The stranger raised a disdainful eyebrow at Harley's cell phone. "New name or old?" he said.

Harley looked up, puzzled by the question.

"Most of us take a new name when we come here," the man explained. "Represents the change—darkness to light, slavery to freedom, that kind of thing." He shrugged. "The kids love it. They get to name themselves after plants, ancient heroes, high-sounding concepts—anything to show they're different from who they were before they came here."

Callaway thought of the young man telling Gardenia that someone named "Freedom" was going into labor. He had a feeling "Freedom" wasn't the name on the mother's birth certificate.

"Anyway," the man went on, waving his hand, "you can call me Jed."

Callaway raised his eyebrows. "Is that your real name?"

"Jedediah Everett Landon. Actually, I don't have a new name. Most of the kids just call me 'Carpenter Joe.'"

Landon pulled out a chair and slumped into it. "The point I was trying to make is that when we have a problem, we work it out ourselves. There's always a way to do things peacefully."

"That didn't work out so well for this woman," Harley said, holding up her phone so that Landon could get a better look at the victim's picture.

"Oh, Sienna," Landon murmured with a heavy shake of his head. "You were never ready for this world."

Callaway detected a note of genuine regret in the man's voice. "How did you know the victim?"

"She lived not far from here, just down Sawyer Pass. She was pretty involved with the community, so I saw her now and then."

"What did you mean, she was never ready for this world?" Harley said.

Landon pawed a lock of hair away from his face. "I mean she was too innocent, too naive. Always trusting the wrong people." He glanced from Callaway to Harley, then back again. "You going to tell me what happened to her?"

"Someone killed her," Callaway answered. "Dumped her body at the side of the road."

Landon lowered his head and began rubbing at his face. "Well, can't say as I'm terribly surprised."

This caught Callaway's interest. "Why's that?"

"Humans are pack animals. We've survived as a species because we've found ways to work together. That's what this whole community is about: everyone contributing so the whole is more than the sum of its parts. Like a big family."

"And how does this relate to the victim?"

Landon sighed. "Sienna was one of the founders of Holy Hope. She planted the first gardens, showed everyone what crops to rotate and how to keep the soil fertile and balanced. She had quite the green thumb."

Callaway thought of the victim's floral tattoos. He glanced at Harley, who was busy furiously taking notes on her phone. He thought of how she had smoothly transitioned from one detail to the next back at the crime scene, and how her analysis had led them here, to Holy Hope. She was a natural. She worked too damn hard not to be.

"It was a real loss when she left," Landon continued. "We all felt it. She was definitely one of the good ones."

"When did she leave?" Harley asked.

Jed cocked one eye at the ceiling. "She left here...oh...maybe six months ago? She didn't go far, mind you—just up the hill, you might say. Built her own place over on Sawyer Pass."

"So she was still living off-grid?" Callaway said, surprised someone would leave the community but not the lifestyle. Sawyer Pass was many miles from any telephone or water lines. "Why'd she leave the community?"

Landon waved his hand in the air dismissively. "Oh, something about being agnostic. Didn't like that some of us are people of faith.

We don't believe in the Flying Spaghetti Monster or anything like that, if that's what you're wondering. But there's something spiritual about the wilderness, about living close to the land. A sense of mystery, know what I mean?"

Callaway nodded. He did not consider himself a religious man, despite his Catholic upbringing, but hiking deep into the wilderness always made him feel close to the infinite, like he was touching a grand mystery he couldn't quite grasp.

"Where did you say she lived?" Harley said.

Landon gestured, as if they could see through the wall. "Just up the road. Go back the way you came, take the first left. You'll see it. Not much down that road but old farmhouses, most of them relics left by the first settlers."

Callaway made a mental note to check it out.

"Has anyone else left recently?" he said.

Landon's lips pressed together in a hesitant frown. "Look," he said, "you're going to make it into this big thing. 'People Flee Holy Hope in Droves'—something like that. You know the saying about not shitting where you live?"

Callaway spoke as reassuringly as he could. "I promise you, Mr. Landon, we're not here to write headlines. We just want to find out what happened to Sienna."

Landon sighed. "There was another woman, yes. Eleanor Renfrew. She and Sienna lived together."

"I'm sorry," Harley interrupted. "What was Sienna's last name again?"

"Davis. Sienna Davis."

Harley glanced at Callaway and gestured questioningly at her phone. Callaway nodded, letting her know he would be fine on his own if she wanted to make a call. She stepped outside.

As the door closed behind Harley, Callaway dragged a second chair across the packed floor. He sat down, hunching forward with his hat clutched in his hands. He felt like a gorilla in a child's playhouse.

"And they both went missing around the same time?" he said.

"That's correct."

"Any idea where Eleanor might have gone?"

Landon stared thoughtfully at the floor. "Well, they were both involved in selling produce—beets, potatoes, sweet peppers, that kind of thing. That's how most of us make money to pay taxes and all: we sell things. The road leading up here isn't exactly the 405, so sometimes we find rides into town. Sienna and Eleanor have a farmer friend who likes to give them rides to the local market—he has a thing for them, you ask me."

"You got a name for this friend?"

"Gale Underwood." He spoke the name carefully, then nodded. "Yeah, that's it. Young guy. He's one of the newer members here. Most of us don't have automobiles, but Gale kept his. Seems like he's got one foot on each side of the fence, in my opinion."

Landon leaned back and began rubbing his lips, his eyes cutting to the side before darting back to Callaway's. Recalling a class on body language he had once taken for the agency, Callaway felt certain Landon was holding something back. The question was, what?

"Anything more I should know about Gale?" he said.

"You should probably ask him. We weren't close." He gestured with his hand, then went back to rubbing his lips. His knee began to bounce.

Callaway sighed and leaned back in his chair, which creaked beneath him. The back was too short, the contours too rigid. He was going to need a chiropractor if he sat there much longer.

"Listen, Joe," he began. "You cared about Sienna, right?"

Landon nodded, his eyebrows pulling together suspiciously. "Yeah..." The word was part-answer, part-question.

"So why are you protecting someone who might know what happened to her?"

Landon stood suddenly and crouched over the fire, his back to Callaway. "I'm not protecting him," he insisted. "I just don't know the guy, okay? Whatever he did, that's his business, not mine."

Callaway cocked his head, unsure whether he was following. "But if he had something to do with Sienna's death, that's *my* business. You don't want a killer to go free, do you?"

"I'm not talking about that," Landon answered quickly, then shook his head. He rose and leaned against the wall, folding his arms. He sighed, closing his eyes and tipping his head up toward the ceiling.

"Then what are you talking about?" Callaway pressed.

"His past," Landon replied. "Before he came here. We all have a past, right? And some of it's bad. I want you to find whoever killed Sienna, I do, but I don't—"

"But you're more concerned with saving your own ass," Callaway interrupted, his voice a low, dangerous rumble. He rose and took a step toward Landon, whose eyes widened.

"Listen to me very carefully," Callaway said in that same tone, like thunder on the horizon. "I don't give a damn what petty crimes you

22

committed before you came here. But if you don't tell me everything you know about Gale Underwood, I'm going to give a damn. And I'm going to start digging, and if I find so much as an unpaid parking ticket on your record, so help me God—"

"Okay!" Landon exclaimed, throwing up his hands. "He was in the National Guard, alright? I don't know what he did, but there was one time we were fishing and he told me he's not allowed to own a firearm any more. Swear to God."

"He told you that?"

Jed nodded and licked his lips, which seemed to have suddenly gone dry. "Who ever heard of that? Ex-military, and you can't own a gun?"

"Dishonorably discharged," Callaway murmured, taking a step back. "Any idea when he'll be back?"

Landon shrugged. "When the market closes. Usually around six or seven."

Callaway nodded to himself. Yes, they would need to have a conversation with Gale Underwood—a long one, perhaps. Even if he hadn't murdered Sienna Davis, there was a good chance he'd been one of the last people to see her alive.

He glanced at Landon, who was watching him warily as if he thought Callaway might throw a punch for good measure.

Callaway pulled a card from his breast pocket and handed it to Landon. "You think of anything else, you give me a call." He paused. "You *do* have a phone, don't you?"

Landon rolled his eyes. "No, I'll light a signal fire. We're survivalists, not troglodytes." Then, deflating a little, he added, "We keep a phone in the Big House for emergencies."

The Big House. The term struck Callaway as odd, like a holdover from the days of slavery. Before his curiosity could compel him to ask which house Landon was referring to, however, the door opened and Harley poked her head in.

"How's it going in here?" she said. There was an excited shine to her eyes that suggested she had news.

"Just finished," Callaway answered. He gave Landon a nod, then ducked through the doorway.

Landon followed. "And try to be discreet?" he said. "I don't need anyone knowing I talked to you."

Callaway set his hat on his head and turned around, smiling in the afternoon sunshine. "Mum's the word. And don't forget to call if you think of anything else. I wouldn't want to have to trouble you again."

Landon grumbled something and closed the door.

"Looks like you made a new friend," Harley observed.

"Some people just need a little incentive to do the right thing, that's all."

Callaway started walking toward the road, Harley falling in step beside him. The fresh air felt wonderful after the stuffiness of the hut.

"I had Ray do some digging on our victim," Harley said, referring to a tech-savvy consultant employed on an as-needed basis by the Santa Fe field office. He had helped them gain access to the victims' phones in the Navarro case, which had proved crucial to the investigation.

"Get this," Harley continued, her voice animated. "Two years ago, Sienna Davis was living with her husband and two sons out by El Paso, just a regular homemaker who liked to bake peach pies for the minister and host book club for the ladies. Then one day she goes missing— takes the car and leaves in the middle of the day while the boys are playing in the backyard."

As they passed the pinyon pines, Holy Hope opened up before them again. Several boys were standing in the back of Callaway's truck, pretending to shoot at the children still on the ground.

"So how'd she end up here?" Callaway replied, watching as one of the older boys began jumping up and down, rocking the bed of the truck.

"That's the mystery," Harley answered. "According to a childhood friend of hers, a school teacher by the name of Lindsay Mack who grew up with Sienna in Iowa, Sienna wasn't as happy as her husband wanted everyone to believe."

"That would explain the scars on her wrist," Callaway observed. "Ms. Mack is still in Iowa, then?"

Harley nodded. "She claims Sienna got 'disillusioned' about the life she was living and began talking about starting over somewhere else. She wanted to 'get away from it all.'"

"I'd say this counts," Callaway observed as they neared the truck. One by one, the boys noticed the agents and their smiles fell. The children watched them with silent, curious faces.

"Come on, kids," Gardenia called from the side of the road, a basin in her hands. "Our guests were just leaving." She smiled at the agents, but there was something mechanical about the expression. She reminded Callaway of the nuns back in Catholic school, but he wasn't sure why.

Callaway gave her a polite wave as he opened the driver side door. She stayed where she was a few moments longer, then tossed the contents of the basin into a patch of cabbages. Dark, brownish liquid splashed up against the leaves.

"What else did you learn from your new BFF?" Harley said.

Callaway watched in the mirror as the children dispersed, hurrying off to cause mischief elsewhere. "According to Landon, Sienna was living nearby with a woman named Eleanor Renfrew, who also seems to have gone missing."

"Sounds like we should head over and check out the house."

Callaway took a deep breath and released it slowly through his teeth. "The thing is, Landon claims there's this farmer, Gale Underwood, who's been giving Sienna and Eleanor rides into town. National Guard, dishonorable discharge."

"Discharged for what?"

Callaway shrugged. "Not sure."

"Well, it's your turn to call Ray. I can't talk with him without the conversation getting around to dinner and drinks."

Callaway grinned. "You cougar, you. You should be ashamed of yourself, flirting with a man half your age."

Harley rolled her eyes. "You were talking about this Underwood character?" she prompted.

"He should be back this evening—six or seven, Landon said. I'm thinking we wait him out."

"You don't think we've overstayed our welcome a bit? It's...what...four o'clock? We could head over to Ms. Renfrew's place and be back with plenty of time to spare."

Callaway pressed his lips together reluctantly. "And what if Underwood comes back early? He might hear we've been asking around and decide to run. It's too risky."

"And the other risk," Harley answered, "is that Ms. Renfrew is in trouble, and we're doing nothing to help her. Do you really want to sit here for the next few hours knowing she could be with Sienna's killer right now?"

Callaway stared out the windshield, wearily rubbing his forehead. He didn't like the idea of waiting any more than Harley did, but neither could he stomach the possibility of letting Underwood escape their grasp simply because they got impatient.

Maybe this is what got her into hot water, he thought. *Her damned impatience.*

He was still debating what to do when his phone buzzed. He mouthed "Newbury" to Harley as he answered it.

"What can I do for you, boss?" he said.

25

Newbury's baritone voice was as dry as corn husks after harvest. "Where are you?"

"We're over at Holy Hope Community, following up on a lead connected to that homicide victim we found this morning."

"We?"

Callaway glanced at Harley, who was studying his face attentively. "Agent Cole couldn't help herself. I tried to convince her she needed to set boundaries, but she insisted she didn't want to wait till Monday."

Harley gave him the finger. He grinned.

"That's good," Newbury answered without a touch of humor. "How's she doing?"

"Diving in with both feet. You know how she is—no half measures with this one."

Harley crossed her arms and raised her eyebrows at him, as if to say, *You done having fun at my expense?*

"And the investigation?" Newbury pressed in that same formal, nothing-but-the-facts tone. "Got a name on our victim yet?"

"Sienna Davis. Went missing from her home in El Paso about two years ago. Turns out she was living on the outskirts of Holy Hope with a woman by the name of Eleanor Renfrew. There's a local farmer who gives them rides into town—we're waiting for him to get back."

"Good work." He paused. "But I'm afraid...to..." The words became garbled.

Callaway sat forward. "Sorry, boss, you're cutting out. Run that by me again?"

"I had the same problem," Harley said. "No service out here. Dropped the call several times."

After a few moments, Newbury's voice broke through again. "—hear me now?"

"Loud and clear."

"I was saying I'm going to have to redirect you."

Callaway waited, surprised.

"A second body's just been found," Newbury finished.

"Shit," Callaway muttered, shaking his head. He had hoped the murder would prove a one-off, a crime of passion committed by a reckless killer likely to leave plenty of breadcrumbs behind him. But two bodies, especially at two different locations, suggested this case might be a bit more complicated than he had planned for.

"What is it?" Harley whispered, but Callaway shook his head at her, still focused on the conversation with Newbury.

"And what about our suspect?" he said.

"Unless you have damning evidence," Newbury replied, "your suspect can wait. I need you over on Lovers' Lane as soon as possible. Local PD are roping the area off, but you know how easy it is to muck up a crime scene."

Callaway frowned, his mind caught on that name. "Wait, did you say Lovers' Lane?"

"You know it?"

"It's less than ten miles from here."

"Then it shouldn't take you long to get there."

"Sounds good, boss. We'll keep you posted."

Callaway ended the call. He stared at the phone, still frowning.

Harley cleared her throat loudly, raising her eyebrows in expectation. "Want to fill me in?" she said.

Callaway's voice was low, sober. "Just found a second body," he answered as he started the truck. "Out on Lovers' Lane. Not much out that way but pastureland."

Harley said nothing as they swung around and drove past the blank, staring faces of the residents of Holy Hope. The children were nowhere to be seen. As they passed an unmarked dirt road on the left, the one Landon had claimed would take them to the house Sienna Davis had shared with Eleanor Renfrew, Harley made an observation that had already been swirling around in Callaway's mind.

"First Coyote Creek, then Lovers' Lane," she said. "The killer's close, Callaway."

He nodded, clenching his jaw. "Right under our noses."

CHAPTER FIVE

Skink closed the tailgate and hung his head, panting for breath. A thrill of triumph, of invincibility, coursed like electricity through his body.

Won't have to hear from her *again,* he thought, grinning at a hedgehog cactus growing up from the dry earth at his feet. *It's about time she shut her mouth for good.*

It had seemed sacred, the first time he took a life, like walking into church as a child and staring up at the stained glass windows, hearing the stentorian voice of the priest ringing off all that gold and silver. A blissful quiet had washed over him, and for a while he had thought he had escaped the voices for good.

After all, there was no silence like the grave. The dead could not bother the living, could they?

Oh, yes, we can, a cold, mocking voice answered. *We're not done with you, you little punk, not by a longshot.*

Skink groaned. He knew it was true. They had found new bodies and returned to torment him, which was why he'd been forced to kill again. And he would keep on killing for as long as it took to silence them, because he knew they would not leave him alone until he did.

You're pathetic, the voice whispered. *A waste of space. Why don't you drown yourself in the toilet and do the world a favor?*

Skink struck the tailgate with his fist, denting the metal. "Leave me alone!" he growled. "Why won't you just leave me alone?"

Make me, the voice answered. *If you've got the guts.*

Skink clutched the tailgate with all his strength as he felt a fit coming on. That was what Momma had always called them, back before her boyfriend whisked her off to Las Vegas: "the fits." It started as a twitch in his wrist. When he stopped it there, it moved to his lips, his mouth forming words he could not – or perhaps did not wish to – say aloud.

Stop, he moaned inwardly. *Please, no more.*

He felt the sting of the broom swiping across his face.

You pathetic little skink! What's wrong with you? You're such a faker!

Was he faking? Was his body under his own control? He did not know.

His head began to shake side-to-side—just a small tremor, a bodily protest against the accusations ringing in his ears. Then a memory would come into sharp relief, and with it a stab of physical pain. His body would shiver, as if cold, and his head would give a violent jerk.

He sank helplessly to the ground.

Get up, you maggot! You worthless piece of shit!

"No, no, no," he murmured, shaking more violently now. He had screwed up. He should have waited until he had both in his sights rather than taking them one at a time. Now the second would be wary. Now she would be ready. And the voices would not be silent until both were dealt with.

You don't think I can see right through you? Skink! Why don't you go crawl back into your hole?

A thrumming pain was growing in his head. Beads of sweat ran down his ribcage. If only he could go back, if only he could do it *right* this time…

Then a sound cut across the hillside, two syllables shouted on a loud clarion of a voice. A *name*. The darkness ate up the sound like a greedy tapeworm.

Immediately Skink's shaking stopped. He sat up, his mind clearing with a sense of rejuvenation. Yes, there was still a way to do it right, still a way to silence both of them for good. The answer was coming right to him.

The voice called again, summoning Skink to action. A thrill of excitement filled him as he rose and peered up the shadowy slope.

The only question was…where was she?

He would have to go to her. He could not risk her turning back.

He climbed the slope in long, purposeful strides. He was a creature of the wilderness, a natural-born hunter. His sharp eyes cut across the dark landscape.

At last he spotted the figure. She was limping down the slope, glancing about in desperation as she called out the name. But the woman she called would not answer, oh no. Skink had made sure of that.

He smiled, pleased with this secret knowledge. Confident they were alone, he stepped down hard on a branch. It cracked underfoot, and the woman turned her head, her mouth and eyes open in shock.

"What do you want?" she said, mustering a note of annoyance. It was not enough, however, to hide the delicious throb of fear thrumming like an artery beneath the words. Oh, how Skink loved the sound.

He stood there, saying nothing, watching her the way one might watch a movie. His mouth hung slack in the intensity of his focus as he wondered if she knew what evil spirit was inside her, burrowed there like a grub in the side of a tree.

The woman's eyes cast about, as if deciding where she might go. "I'm looking for a friend of mine. Have you seen anyone out here?"

Again, Skink kept his silence. He liked seeing her squirm.

The woman took a deep breath, cupped her hands over her mouth, and shouted the name.

"She can't hear you," Skink said. Now that he had found her, he didn't like her shouting any more. It might bring an unwanted visitor, someone who had nothing to do with what was about to happen here.

"What do you mean?" she replied, a tremor in her voice.

"Why don't you come with me? I can show you where she is."

The woman stared at him, unease etched in her features. "Did you do something to her? Did you hurt her?"

Skink grinned. "Come and see."

She stared for several seconds, a classic deer-in-the-headlights' pose: eyes wide, body tense as a bowstring. Then she did the very thing Skink had been waiting for.

She ran.

A delicious sense of power washed over Skink. Now he was the one in control. Like a dog excited by the chase, he ran after her.

Oh, it was good to be alive.

CHAPTER SIX

Harley's chest tightened at the sight of the woman flung like a ragdoll on the side of the dirt road. The victim lay on her right side, the earth and weeds beneath her stained with blood. Her ribcage was partially collapsed, her hip fractured, her head resting at an odd angle that suggested several broken vertebrae. Though Harley had seen plenty of bodies in her eleven years with the Bureau, the sight of one – especially one mangled as badly as the body before her now – could still hit her like a gallon of cold water.

Harley glanced up as Callaway approached, leaving his conversation with a farmer in bib overalls and a scraggly gray beard who had called in the body. Behind him stood a produce truck packed to the gills with heads of lettuce, beets, spinach, and numerous other locally-grown vegetables. Harley gave the front of the truck a cursory glance, wondering briefly whether there was any chance he was the one who had hit the victim. She saw no blood, damage, or any other indication the truck had been involved.

"Says he was looking at the flowers, thinking of picking a few for his wife," Callaway explained, jabbing a thumb over his shoulder to indicate the farmer. "That's why the road is called Lovers' Lane, after all: the colors. You should see the aspen in the fall."

Harley looked up at the thin forest covering the hillside to her left. Not far up that hill was the house Sienna and Eleanor had lived in, which in turn was close to Holy Hope—the very community where a man named Gale Underwood lived. Coyote Creek Road, where Sienna Davis's body had been found, was not far south.

"And don't worry," Callaway added. "I gave his truck a casual once-over. Nothing on that grille but dead bugs."

"Could be a hit-and-run," Harley observed. "What makes Newbury think this is connected to our case?"

"Besides the lack of brake marks and the proximity to the first body?" Callaway jerked his head at the farmer. "Guy who came across the body, he says he recognized her. Want to guess the name?"

Harley's heart sank. "Don't tell me it's Ms. Renfrew."

Callaway nodded with a look of grim satisfaction. "The very same. Quite a coincidence, don't you think?"

31

Harley felt a familiar sense of pressure beginning to build. It would continue to build as long as the investigation continued, and there was no way to release it but to find the killer or shelve the case for good. The pressure created a sense of urgency now, but she knew that in the long run it would prove exhausting if the case were to go on for months or years without resolution, as some cases did.

Sinking to her haunches, Harley studied the swath of purple yarrow flowers blooming around the body. "I don't see any footprints," she observed. "If I wanted someone dead, I wouldn't just hit them with my truck and then drive on, hoping for the best."

"Maybe he stopped at the side of the road, watched to see if she got up. When it became obvious she was down for the count, he booked it."

Harley pressed her lips together in an expression of skepticism. "Still looks like panic to me. It's sloppy, just like the first body."

"We're ignoring the obvious question here. How did she end up on the side of the road in the first place? Let's assume for a moment Underwood is our guy. He picks the two women up, then—what? Gets a little too friendly with them?"

"No obvious signs of sexual assault on either victim," Harley replied, "though we'll have to wait for the ME's reports to know for sure. A predator would isolate one of the women—it's too risky to try anything with both of them. Maybe Eleanor ran."

"But how did she get all the way out here? Landon said Underwood gave them rides to Tejada. That's...what? Twenty miles? No way she ran back."

Harley shook her head. They could spend all day trying to solve the puzzle, but without more pieces, it was little more than an exercise in futility. Meanwhile the killer was on the loose—destroying evidence, inventing an alibi, perhaps even selecting another target.

She moved closer to the body. Several dried leaves clung to the victim's clothes, which looked like they could have been made at Holy Hope just like Sienna Davis's, and small scratches marked her arms and cheeks. One shoe was missing, revealing a sockless, dirty foot. The remaining sneaker was crusted with dried mud.

Harley studied the victim's neck. "No bruising, not that I can see. But look at all the scratches."

"Must have come running down from the forest," Callaway murmured.

Harley stared up at the trees as new possibilities surfaced in her mind. "Maybe he attacks them at home. Eleanor escapes, but he strangles Sienna. Then, after dumping the body, he comes back for Eleanor, finds her on the side of the road."

She waited, but Callaway said nothing. He was still staring up at the forest. Harley had the impression, however, that his mind was elsewhere.

"It's a working theory, at least," she added. "Might explain the time difference."

She stepped back, trying to imagine the scene:

Eleanor, scared for her life, stumbles across the road as a vehicle approaches. It's not dark yet, but the shadows are lengthening. Eleanor is exhausted from her descent down the slope, terrified after being attacked in her home, perhaps even feeling guilty for leaving Sienna to deal with the killer alone. She needs to find help, and for a moment, as the vehicle barrels toward her—

"What's the speed limit here?" she wondered aloud. "Fifty-five?"

She waited. When Callaway didn't answer, she turned toward him, crunching sand beneath her shoe. He was looking at her strangely.

"You never told me about the Kavers case," he said.

The words struck Harley as a complete non sequitur. What did the Kavers case have to do with this one? And why in the world was he asking now, when they could be so close to the killer?

Unsure what to say, Harley returned her attention to the body, searching for anything she might have missed before. Something was nagging at her, but she wasn't sure what.

"It's a simple question," Callaway added.

"Are you telling me you didn't get curious and read the report?"

"I did, actually," Callaway answered.

"Well, there you go. Anything you need to know is in there."

He was silent for several seconds, an unseen presence behind her. She hoped he would drop it—this wasn't the time for discussing the methods and merits of past cases. They needed to stay focused.

"I'm not talking about *your* investigation," he continued. "I'm talking about the OPR's investigation."

Harley closed her eyes and sighed. She should have known this was coming eventually. No good deed went unpunished, after all.

"I didn't bring it up before," Callaway continued in that slow, determined way of his, "because you were just a consultant. But if I'm going to be working with you on a more…*permanent* basis, I need to know just what kind of person I'm dealing with."

Harley's gaze moved up and down the victim's body, roving. "Whether you can rely on me, you mean?"

He ignored this. "What were they investigating, Harley? Specifically, I mean. The OPR doesn't get involved unless the Bureau has good reason to believe an agent stepped out of line. If there's something I need to be aware of, here's your chance. I can't trust you if you're not willing to be straight with me."

She rose and turned, feeling suddenly as if she was on trial. "What about when we were in those tunnels with Felix Navarro?" she answered edgily. "You seemed to have no trouble trusting me then."

"That was different. I had no choice but to trust you."

"And what a disaster that was." She shook her head and began moving along the side of the road.

Would the witch hunt never end? Was Newbury the only one who realized how instrumental she had been in putting Kavers away—and how easily another agent might have mucked it up by playing by the rules? She was the one who had taken the risks, put her career on the line to stop the killings. Had her methods jeopardized the investigation, she would have received all the blame. So why didn't she get any credit for succeeding?

"Where are you going?" Callaway said, following her. He sighed, his voice growing conciliatory. "Look, this isn't a one-way street. If there's anything you think you need to know about me, I'm an open book. You want to hear why I became a cop? Want to know about my family?"

"I've heard it all before," she said, fanning the roadside weeds with her hand.

He stopped. "I haven't told you—not all of it."

"You don't have to." She faced him. "You became a cop because of some old injustice—childhood friend got picked up by the wrong stranger, isn't that what you said?"

"Hitchhiking," he added, watching her warily.

"And so you became a cop to make a difference. It scratched the itch for a while, but you wanted to do more than hand out tickets and direct traffic. So when an FBI recruiter came by, you jumped at the chance. How am I doing so far?"

"Go on," he said.

She kept walking as the details gathered in her mind. "You were older at this point, probably going steady with a college sweetheart. She was ready to start a family, and you thought you were, too." Here she sensed some of her own history bleeding into the narrative, but she went on anyway.

34

"At first it was great," she continued, once again searching the weeds. "Crime-fighter by day, family man by night. They complemented one another well—until they didn't. You're still playing for both teams, but pretty soon you'll realize you have to make a choice."

"You think you have me figured out, don't you?"

She sighed. "I'm a profiler, Callaway. It's what I do—I study people."

"Yeah, well, you're wrong," he said with a touch of anger. "I met my wife at a kickboxing class, not in college, and I applied to the Bureau after a criminal justice seminar. No recruiter's pitch needed."

She noticed what she was looking for and squatted down, parting the weeds. A white sneaker lay on its side in the dirt.

"And I'm happily married with two kids, thank you very much," he continued. "Just because you couldn't balance work and home doesn't mean I'm doomed to the same fate."

She ignored the jab. "Gloves," she said, holding out her hand.

Callaway, who kept a box of plastic gloves in his truck, handed her a pair.

"What happened during the Kavers case?" he said softly.

She photographed the sneaker with her phone, then hooked two fingers and a thumb around the back of the shoe, raising it in the air. It was caked in mud, just like the first shoe.

Callaway shadowed her as she returned to the body, where she held the shoe up to the victim's foot.

"It's too big," she murmured. "At least two sizes too large, I'd say. Why would Eleanor have worn shoes that were too big for her? And where did the mud come from?"

Callaway said nothing. The silence began to congeal. She didn't like ignoring him, but what business of his was the OPR investigation? If they decided she had acted in a manner unfitting for an agent of the Bureau, they would hand down consequences. If not, what was there to talk about?

Finally, Harley sighed. "I don't want to talk about it, okay? When the OPR files their report, if there's anything to report, you can read all about it then. Otherwise…" She trailed off.

Callaway gave her a cool stare. She felt bad about keeping him at arm's length, but she couldn't have him questioning her every decision, not now.

She was still deciding whether she should say something more when her phone vibrated. The suave, self-assured voice of Ray

Ranganathan, the same young techie she had called earlier to look into Sienna Davis's background, filled her ear as she answered.

"What's up, Harley? You and Joker out walking the beat?"

Harley passed a weary hand over her eyes. Talking with Ray had a way of sapping her energy.

"You get it?" he pressed. "Your name's Harley, so that makes him—"

"Do you need something, Ray?"

It took him only a moment to recover. That was Ray's superpower: the ability to remain almost entirely unaffected in the face of near-constant rejection.

"Yeah, I've been trying to reach you. First I thought you were ignoring my calls—building the suspense, so to speak. But then I realized it's probably just because you're way out in the boonies. Not many cell towers out that way."

She cocked her head, puzzled. "How do you know where we are, Ray? You consult for the Bureau—you're not briefed on the whereabouts of agents."

Ray's hesitation was brief, but telling. "I overheard a conversation, that's all. Water-cooler talk."

"You're a bad liar, Ray. How are you tracking us?"

"Using your phones, is all. Really, it amazes me more people don't do it."

Harley thought about the near-total absence of modern technology at Holy Hope. Maybe they were on to something.

"Most people aren't that nosy," she answered. She glanced over at Callaway, who was staring off into the distance, his expression stony.

"Listen, Ray," she said, "I'm in the middle of something here. So unless you have something important—"

"Holy shit, are you at a crime scene?"

"Ray, I'm going to hang up now."

"Wait, wait, wait! I was calling to say I ran that name for you. Uh…" His chair creaked, as if he were leaning forward to read something. "Gale Underwood."

"Anything interesting?"

"No hits—not anyone in the National Guard. Well, except for this one guy who died about eight years ago, but I'm guessing that's not helpful."

"Good guess," Harley replied dryly. She paused, wondering what to make of this news. As always, Ray was quick to fill the silence.

"So I was thinking," he said. "I've been doing this gig for about four months now, but the boss man still won't give me an answer about a full-time role. Think you could talk with him, use some of that feminine charm you have in abundance?"

"You know I'm old enough to be your mother, right?"

"And yet you don't look a day over twenty. How do you do it, Harley Quinn? Is it cool if I call you Harley Quinn?"

"Goodbye, Ray." She ended the call before he could respond. If the FBI thing didn't work out for Ray, he could always become a phone salesman—*if* he could avoid the harassment lawsuits.

"That was Ray," she said to Callaway. "No results for Gale Underwood, not for anyone with a service record with the National Guard. So unless Mr. Landon is lying to us…"

Harley couldn't think of any motive Jedediah Landon would have to lie. If he took issue with their investigation, he could have simply refused to talk with them, like everyone else. No, Landon seemed to care about Sienna. He had no reason to throw them off the scent.

"Gale Underwood is a fake name," Callaway finished. There was a coolness to his gaze that suggested their earlier conversation wasn't over yet. Harley knew he could set it aside for the moment, but sooner or later she would have to open up if she wanted to earn his trust.

"Fake name," Callaway mused, "dishonorable discharge from the National Guard. It's not looking good for Gale."

Harley nodded, liking Underwood for the killings more and more. "Where did Landon say that farmers market was?"

CHAPTER SEVEN

Harley plucked a few bills from her wallet and passed them to the elderly Apache woman seated beneath an umbrella. The woman's slight smile set in motion a series of wrinkles, rippling back to her ears like waves.

"My sister used to love these," Harley explained to Callaway as she picked up the pair of beaded earrings. Bands of turquoise alternated with white, red, and black, like sunset and coastal waters. "She was always interested in the history of the land, especially before it was settled."

Smiling at the Apache woman, she turned and studied the rows of stalls around her. The Tejada farmers market met a few times a year and brought in sellers from as far as Austin, Texas. Many skilled artisans attended, displaying sculptures made of basswood and butternut, hand-painted ceramics, dream-catchers, grass-fed meats not regulated by the FDA.

And, of course, fruits and vegetables, like the ones Underwood – or whatever his real name was – sold.

"You wear the necklace for her, too?" Callaway said as they ventured deeper into the market, searching for the produce stands. Already some of the sellers were packing their wares into trucks, SUVs, and campers. Soon the area would go back to being just another piece of state land off the highway.

"Most men aren't very observant of a woman's jewelry," Harley said. She spoke from personal experience. More than once, she had worn a particular piece of jewelry just for Rob, and he had completely failed to notice.

"It's my job to notice the details," Callaway answered. "Besides, I'm not most men." His eyes were hidden by his sunglasses, but the slow pivot of his head from side-to-side told Harley only half his attention was on their conversation. The other half was searching for Underwood—not that they had any idea what he looked like. They would have to ask around.

"I'd say most men feel the same way," Harley observed, studying Callaway askance. He radiated coolness like a block of ice. She sensed he wasn't going to forget the way she had ignored his questions earlier, nor would he let it stop him from bringing up the subject again. She supposed he had every right to ask about the investigation, but she also had every right to tell him in her own time and in her own way.

She pulled up short as a pair of children, a boy and a girl, raced across her path. The girl, a few inches taller than the boy, lofted a one-eyed teddy bear high in the air, her face smug with triumph. The boy chased after, his mouth twisted in a silent wail.

"Anthony of Padua," she said as she fell in step beside Callaway again. "Patron Saint of Missing Persons. The necklace, I mean."

"Still miss her?"

"Every day."

Callaway nodded. "They say time heals all wounds, but it's not true. It would probably be more accurate to say dementia heals all wounds."

"What happened to your friend?" she said, regretting now how she had spoken to him back at the crime scene. "The one who was hitchhiking?"

Instead of answering, Callaway gestured at a pair of figures, man and woman, packing pots into the back of a minivan, their hands and wrists brown with clay. A decal on the side of the minivan showed an overlapping pair of capital *H*s twisted with vines.

"Holy Hope," Callaway observed. "I remember seeing that van on our drive in."

"Looks like Sienna and Eleanor weren't the only two Holy Hopers coming here," Harley replied, noticing how Callaway had completely ignored her question. "What do you say we ask if they've seen Underwood?"

Before Callaway could respond, however, a nearby voice said, "Are you talking about Gale?"

They turned to see a bearded giant of a man packing hand blown glass figurines into a cooler. The back of his right hand was scarred white—an occupational hazard, no doubt.

"That's right," Harley answered, wondering if this might be the man they were searching for. "Is he still here?"

The man straightened. His eyes traveled slowly down to her feet, then back up to her face. There was nothing lustful in his stare, only a cool aloofness.

"What's a girl like you doing all the way out here?" he said. "You a tourist?"

"Actually I spent eighteen years of my life around here," Harley answered, rankled by the suggestion. Why did everyone treat her like an outsider? Was it the way she dressed?

Callaway took a step forward and held up his badge. "FBI. We need to speak with Gale Underwood, and we'd appreciate it if you could point us in the right direction."

The stranger's eyes lingered a few seconds longer on Harley before he turned his attention to Callaway. He made a soft clucking sound at the sight of the badge.

"Must have done something bad," he said, "for a Fed to come looking."

"Two Feds, actually," Harley corrected. She didn't like the way the man had turned his body away from her, as if deliberately excluding her from the conversation. As if she didn't belong at the same table as the grownups.

"So what was it?" he said to Callaway in a conspiratorial whisper, ignoring Harley. "He kill someone? Rob a train? Shit, I knew that man was destined for trouble first time I saw him."

It was a curious phenomenon to Harley. Some people, when told they'd been living next to a serial killer for the past decade, would go on about how friendly the killer had always seemed. Others, however, would respond with a recitation of suspicions squirreled away over the years, as if taking advantage of the opportunity to vindicate themselves.

"We just need to ask him some questions," Harley said, trying again to insert herself into the conversation.

The stranger answered without looking at her. "Yeah, and I just need to get home in time for supper, but it's tough when I'm standing here talking to you two."

Callaway pulled a ten-dollar-bill from his wallet and slipped it into a tip jar resting on the table. "Does that settle the account?"

The man snorted. "You're gonna have to try a bit harder if you want to move the needle."

Harley began to protest – she was really beginning to tire of this man's intransigence – but Callaway was already rolling up a twenty and stuffing it into the jar.

"There," Callaway said with a friendly smile. "That should compensate you for your time."

In answer, the glass blower jerked his head to the side. "See the bin of squash down the path there, man and woman talking out front? Man's Underwood."

Callaway pinched the brim of his hat. "Much obliged."

"Any time," the man answered, following Harley with his eyes. "Don't be a stranger now, you hear?"

As they moved away, Harley shook her head in frustration. "What was his problem? I might as well have been invisible."

"It's your accent," Callaway said. "Got that Yankee twang. You're going to have to work on it if you want to pass for a local."

"Do I have to be a local to be treated with respect?"

Callaway shrugged. "Around here, you do."

Harley tried to let the incident go as they neared Underwood, who was filling a paper bag with squash while his customer fanned herself with a flier. Underwood was young and lithe, with disheveled red hair and a patterning of freckles across his nose that gave him a boyish look.

It occurred to Harley that she still didn't have her gun, her cuffs, or even her badge. They were waiting for her on Newbury's desk, and she'd been working the investigation with Callaway all day without so much as a break. She hadn't even gone home to change or move into her new house.

Still, she wasn't going to hang back and let Callaway apprehend a suspect alone.

As the woman moved away, cradling the bag of squash against her bosom, Underwood looked up and saw the two approaching agents. His smile froze.

"Gale Underwood?" Callaway said in a light, friendly tone. "Can we talk to you for a minute?"

Underwood glanced down and brushed dust off his shirt. He planted his hands on his hips for a moment, as if considering what to do.

Don't do it, Harley thought as they neared him. *Don't do it.* She could see the tension in his body. He was coiled tight.

A bray of laughter came from Harley's left. She turned to see a middle school boy bent double, hand over his mouth as soda ran between his fingers. Several other boys looked on, pointing and laughing.

"You just shot soda out your nose!" one of them exclaimed, cracking up.

Ignoring the boys, Harley returned her attention to Underwood— just in time to catch a fleeting glimpse of him as he disappeared between two tents.

"Shit!" Harley exclaimed as she and Callaway gave chase.

CHAPTER EIGHT

Why do they always run? Harley thought as she sprinted after Underwood, barely managing to sidestep a stroller pushed into her path by a sixty-something grandmother still staring after the fleeing farmer, her eyes wrinkled in puzzlement. As Harley danced around the stroller, she glanced down to see a pair of twins goggling up at her, one holding a set of plastic keys, the other a cloth book with an owl on the cover.

The baby with the keys held them up toward Harley, mouth open in a round *O*.

Gaining her footing again, Harley pushed off and raced between the pair of tents, emerging on the other side in a crowd of babbling teenagers with ice cream cones in their hands. She pushed through them, ignoring their startled murmurs.

"FBI!" she shouted. "Let me through!"

As she escaped the group, she caught sight of Underwood hurtling a stack of tomato crates. He caught his shoe on a nail, toppling one of the crates and spilling cherry tomatoes across the dirt. He got to his feet and cast an anxious glance over his shoulder, searching for Harley. A man in a sun hat – the tomato seller, presumably – began to remonstrate with Underwood. Underwood shoved the farmer back and kept running.

Harley leapt over the remaining tomato crate and nearly slipped as several tomatoes popped underfoot. The farmer reached for her, his mouth twisted in anger, but she ducked his arm and kept going.

Underwood had doubled back and was now racing through the artisan section of the market, probably heading toward the parking lot at the far end. Harley and Callaway had parked at the opposite side of the market, so if Underwood was indeed running toward a vehicle, they needed to stop him before he reached it.

I sure hope Callaway is calling for backup, she thought. She stole a quick glance over her shoulder but didn't see him. Maybe he had gotten held up.

Harley lowered her head, running for all she was worth. Underwood was fast, but Harley's many hours at the gym began to tell, despite the fact that she hadn't had a single calorie since breakfast.

She was closing the gap.

Then, as Underwood passed a table lined with handmade pottery, Callaway emerged from beneath a canopy, arms outstretched as he dove at Underwood. Like a shifty running back, Underwood planted his heel and twisted away, ducking beneath Callaway's arm.

Callaway landed hard in the dirt and rolled onto his back. As he began to rise, Underwood snatched up a black vase and threw it down at Callaway's head. The agent managed to raise his arm in time, causing the vase to shatter against his arm instead of against his head.

Underwood picked up a second object – this one a decorative clay teapot – and was about to hurl it at Callaway when Harley slipped her arms under his, then wrapped them around the back of his neck, catching him in a full nelson hold. Underwood dropped the teapot and twisted, trying to throw her body, but she adjusted her footing and tightened her grip, bending his neck down toward his chest.

"Shit!" Underwood groaned.

Harley was too tired and pissed off to feel any sympathy. "Keep fighting, see how it feels," she said.

"Okay, okay!" he cried, his body going limp. "Take it easy!"

"You alright, partner?" Harley said to Callaway, who rose and rubbed his forearm, the skin of which had turned an angry red.

"I'll survive," he said, grimacing. "Guess I need to work on my tackling—been a long time since college."

A crowd of murmuring onlookers had begun to gather. Callaway showed them his badge, then pulled out his cuffs as he approached Underwood.

"Want my advice?" Callaway said as he slapped one of the cuffs on Underwood's wrist. "Next time you choose to run, pick a day when she's not already pissed off."

*

Harley leaned back in her chair, making a show of studying a manila folder that was actually no more than a Conduct Policy statement. They were in the interview room of the Huerta County Sheriff's Department, a gray, nondescript room with a hanging fluorescent light protected by a cage, a clock that was five minutes behind, and not much else.

Underwood sat across from her at the table, hands folded across his chest, his head tipped back at a haughty angle. Callaway leaned against the wall, regarding the suspect with a stony stare. A large bruise was swelling on his forearm.

"It's not looking good for you, Gale," Harley said in a tone of regret. "Assaulting a federal officer is bad enough on its own, but on top of the murders..." She shook her head.

Underwood snorted in disgust. "You ain't got nothing on me. I'm clean."

"Yeah?" Harley kept her eyes on the file, as if absorbed in what she was reading. "Then why'd you run? Why'd you assault Agent Callaway with a pot?"

"Bitch assaulted me first," Underwood sneered. "Tried to, anyway. How's that arm feeling, big fella?"

"Want me to test it out?" Callaway replied. "See if it still works?"

"No need for that," Harley interrupted. "We're all adults here, aren't we?"

She didn't worry things would get out of hand – Callaway was too professional to let a punk like Underwood get beneath his skin – but she did want to control the pace. They knew almost nothing about Underwood, and it would stay that way if he clammed up. They had taken his fingerprints, but it would take time to get the results: a week, maybe two. Until then, the only way they were going to learn his real name was if he told them.

Harley cleared her throat. "Let's back up a bit. The reason we wanted to talk to you, Gale—should I call you Gale, or is there another name you prefer?"

He stared back at her, sullen.

"Because from what I hear," she continued, "you served in the National Guard, is that correct?"

Underwood said nothing.

"It's an admirable thing, serving in the military," Harley continued. "Wouldn't you say so, Callaway?"

Callaway stared silently at Underwood.

"It begs the question, though," Harley went on, undeterred by the staring contest. "What happened? You were dishonorably discharged, is that correct?"

"Bullshit," Gale muttered.

"You mean you weren't dishonorably discharged?"

"No, I mean it was a bullshit decision, just like you bringing me in here on some trumped-up charge."

Harley took a moment's pause. She chose her words carefully, not wanting to reveal how little they knew about him.

"What was so trumped-up about the charge?" she said.

"The fact I was innocent, for starters. The fact that the guy who snitched on me was just a kiss-ass looking for attention."

"If it's any consolation," Callaway said, "I'd say there's a promising career for you in Hollywood if the whole farming thing doesn't pan out. You've got the victim role down pat."

"Screw you, man."

Harley shot Callaway a warning glance to tell him he wasn't helping. "What was your side of the story, Gale? How did you see it?"

He stared at her blankly for a few seconds. Then his lips thinned in a greasy smile. "You don't know a damn thing about me, do you? All of this—" He made a vague gesture, indicating the whole room— "is just a bluff to get me to confess to something I didn't do. You don't even know my real name."

"Maybe not," Harley answered, "but we will as soon as those fingerprint results come in. Shouldn't be more than fifteen minutes or so. Want to save us all some time and tell us what we're going to find out anyway?"

Underwood watched her with raised eyebrows, unimpressed.

It was worth a shot, she thought.

She leaned back and cleared her throat. "I'll give you two names I do know: Sienna Davis and Eleanor Renfrew. Ring any bells?"

Underwood's eyes narrowed suspiciously.

"As far as we can tell," Harley continued, "you were the last person to see them alive."

Underwood glanced at Callaway, as if looking for confirmation. "Sienna and Eleanor are *dead?*"

"What kind of vehicle do you drive?" Callaway answered.

This caught Underwood off-guard. "I've got an old Suburban. Why?"

Callaway looked at Harley. "Lots of trunk space in those, wouldn't you say? Lay the back seats down. Could definitely stow a body in there."

Harley's attention was on Underwood, reading his response. He looked incredulous.

"A body?" he said, turning his hands palm-up. "You think *I* killed them?"

There was a beat of silence. Harley kept her eyes on Underwood, looking for any tell to suggest he was lying. His surprise looked genuine. Then again, he might just be a good poker player.

"If the boot fits," Callaway said.

Something about the words stuck in Harley's head. Her mind wandered back to the crime scene, picturing Eleanor Renfrew's body twisted at the side of the road. Something wasn't adding up, but what?

"No way, man," Underwood was saying, growing more animated. "I gave them a ride into town yesterday morning, sure, but that was it. They were both happy and healthy when I left them."

"That was it, huh?" Callaway pressed. "You just left them there, didn't think they might need a ride back?"

He hesitated. Callaway, perhaps sensing his advantage, stepped forward and planted both of his large hands on the table.

"We've got witnesses saying they got back in your vehicle," he said. "We know that much for certain. The question is, where were you taking them?"

It was a lie – they hadn't had enough time to drum up any witnesses – but Callaway sold it well, and the queasy expression on Underwood's face suggested he had bought it. "Okay," he muttered, looking away to avoid Callaway's intense stare. "I drove them back early this morning, so what?"

"That's it? You brought them home, wished them luck, went on your way? Got any witnesses to verify that?"

Underwood swallowed hard. "It wasn't exactly like that. I didn't quite take them all the way home."

Harley could practically see the excitement swelling in Callaway. "No?" he pressed. "You wouldn't have taken a detour down by Coyote Creek Road, would you?"

Underwood's face registered genuine surprise. "Coyote Creek? What would I be doing down there? I dropped them off at Speedy's because I didn't have time to take them home. It's the one just down the road from Holy Hope."

"You expect me to believe you couldn't spare an extra five minutes? What was the big hurry?"

The shoes, Harley thought, frowning at the folder in her hands as her mind moved along a separate track. Why had Eleanor been wearing shoes that didn't fit her? She leaned forward and studied Underwood's sand-colored combat boots. No connection there, not that she could see.

"I was supposed to check in with my parole officer, okay?" Underwood continued, casting a puzzled glance at Harley. "I was already late—five minutes he'll tolerate, but ten?"

This turn seemed to take Callaway off-guard. "And why were you late in the first place?"

"We were up half the night, okay? They were lonely, the two of them living out by themselves. Had some religious issue with the community, so they separated themselves. I took them out to show

46

them a good time."

"What size boots do you wear?" Harley said suddenly.

Both men stared at her, puzzled.

"Elevens," Underwood said. "Why?"

Too big, Harley thought. She waved a hand in the air. "Just clarifying."

Callaway gave her a long look before resuming his line of questioning.

"Were you showing them a good time," he said to Underwood, "or *having* a good time?"

Underwood held up his hands again in an attitude of innocence. "Look, man, it's not like it wasn't consensual. I didn't take advantage of them, and I certainly didn't murder them. You want an alibi? Give my parole officer a call. I can give you his number."

Callaway nodded, withdrawing from the table. "Alright. What is it?"

As Underwood gave Callaway the number, Harley continued to muse over the shoes. Had it been a simple mistake? Had Eleanor grabbed the wrong pair of shoes, perhaps not realizing her mistake until she had already left the house? Could it be as simple as that? If so, why had her feet been so dirty?

Deciding she had no further questions at the moment, Harley stepped out into the hall. Callaway emerged a few moments later, dialing a number into his phone.

"Yes, this is Agent Anthony Callaway with the FBI. We just picked up a man who goes by the name of Gale Underwood, and he claims…"

Callaway's voice faded out as Harley leaned her head against the cool wall and closed her eyes. She imagined the details of the investigation laid out like the pieces of a jigsaw puzzle, but she was too tired to keep trying to fit them together. It had been a long day, and she was running on fumes.

"Bad news," Callaway said to her as he hung up the phone. "Jake's alibi checks out."

"Jake?"

Callaway jerked his head toward the door of the interrogation room. "Jacob Boudoin, dishonorably discharged for sexual assault. His parole officer can testify to being with him from about seven this morning to four this afternoon."

Harley's eyebrows rose. "Nine hours? What were they doing all that time?"

"After the meeting, community service—roadside trash pickup with a crew. Supervised. There's no way he left those bodies."

Harley let out a deep sigh. The news was discouraging, even if she wasn't really surprised.

"Now," Callaway went on, his jaw muscles flexing, "you want to tell me why it was so important to know his shoe size in the middle of my line of questioning?"

"I just can't put it together," she answered. "Almost everyone else at Holy Hope was wearing sandals, Jacob Boudoin excepted. So why was Eleanor wearing a pair of oversized sneakers?"

Callaway planted his hands on his hips and stared at the floor. "Look, it's been a long day. Neither of us has eaten anything since breakfast. What do you say we grab some fast food?"

Harley nodded, knowing a solid meal would do her good.

As they left the precinct, however, she kept thinking about those shoes, wondering what she was missing.

CHAPTER NINE

"Looks like we're back to square one," Harley said as she ruffled through the carton, scavenging the last few French fries at the bottom. "Boudoin is clean."

They sat in Callaway's truck in the middle of a parking lot, a streetlamp casting an orange haze over them. Moths bumped and fluttered around the bulb. Tin foil wrappers, balled napkins, and half-empty sauce packets lay on the seat between them like evidence from a crime scene.

Callaway rolled a drumstick in his fingers, picking out the last few pieces of chicken with his teeth before discarding the bone. He shook his head ruefully as he plucked a fresh napkin.

"Nothing clean about that punk," he said, his upper lip bulging as he worked to free a piece of chicken with his tongue. "But innocent of this crime? Looks that way. Bet he's never been so grateful for his parole officer in his life."

Harley stared out at the dark street. "So what do we do now?" she murmured. "We won't know much until we get the reports back from the ME, but that'll take time, and we don't know if this is an isolated crime or if he'll kill again."

Callaway scooped up the remains of their meal and tossed it into the paper bag, which he then set on the floor between them. He leaned back and rested one wrist on the steering wheel.

"And we won't do any good for anyone if we're exhausted," he said. "We need to get some sleep, look the case over again in the morning with fresh eyes. Might notice something we missed the first time around. There's still plenty of legwork to be done." He ticked off the items with his fingers. "Checking out the victims' house, questioning more of the residents at Holy Hope, waiting for results from the forensics team…" He trailed off.

Harley nodded, but she was not sure she shared his optimism. The day had gone by in a rush of excitement, but all they had to show for it was a pair of bodies and a suspect with a rock-solid alibi. What bothered her most, however, was the word "waiting." There was nothing worse than waiting for a killer to make a mistake, all the while knowing he might take a few more victims along the way.

They both fell silent. It was an uneasy silence full of things unsaid. At last, Harley spoke without preamble.

"John Kavers, age forty-five. No priors, though his teachers did write some interesting things about him when he was in middle school, where he was labeled 'the Creep' by a number of students – mostly girls – for his penchant for running his fingers through their hair when they weren't looking, or sniffing discarded headbands."

Callaway watched her, his eyebrows knitted in solemn interest.

Harley continued, "Intermittent dating life, no relationship ever lasting longer than two or three months. A classic loser: no family ties, little education, minimum-wage job. Handsome, but you wouldn't have known it, given how little effort he put into taking care of himself."

She paused, shuffling through the mental inventory of stored data. Callaway waited.

"First body was found stuffed in a culvert," she continued. "I guess what sticks with me to this day is how young she was, even younger than any of the victims from the Navarro case. Kavers liked them that way. He said they were more malleable, easier to manipulate, but I think that was just the narrative he wanted us to believe."

A note of newfound respect entered Callaway's voice. "You talked with him, face-to-face?"

Harley nodded. "Just him, me, and the tape recorder."

"Why *do* you think he picked such young targets?"

"It was about control, sure—it always is. But in his case, I think it went back to his childhood: single mother, welfare, drug habit, held his hands to the kitchen stove to punish him, that kind of thing. The victims were the same age his mother was when she got pregnant with him, and I think some part of him was punishing her for bringing him into the world, whether or not he was aware he was doing it."

She paused. Talking about the case had cracked open a door to a dark room, one she did not care to reenter. There were monsters in that darkness—John Kavers, yes, but others as well, men in whose eyes Harley had seen a species of evil so pure it was incapable of questioning itself.

"Anyway," she continued, closing the door with an effort, "he led us on a wild goose chase for a while. He was devious—always acted as if the eyes of the world were on him. So he would leave fake clues, mis-directions. Then he graduated to taunting messages."

"I know the kind," Callaway said. "They work in secret but crave the world's attention. How did you get him?"

"A combination of luck and hard work. We discovered the

microfibers on the underside of the sixth victim's purity ring. We matched it to five minivans registered in the area, and we went through the owners of those five vehicles one by one, gradually honing in on Kavers. There was just one problem."

"You didn't have a search warrant," Callaway said.

"That's right. And the judge wasn't going to give us one, not on the evidence we had. 'Too circumstantial,' he said. But Kavers fit the profile to a *t*. He had the time, opportunity, and motive to commit the crimes, and where there's that much smoke, there's bound to be a fire."

She shook her head, recalling how frustrated she'd been. "By the time we had our ducks lined up, though, Kavers would be in the wind. He'd move, invent a new identity for himself, lay low for a while, and then go back to hunting. It had happened before."

"So you searched the van anyway, without the warrant."

She turned her body toward him, curling one leg on the seat. "Wouldn't you? If you knew the man was a murderer – absolutely knew it but just couldn't quite prove it yet – wouldn't you do anything necessary to put him away? Isn't that what we swear we'll do—protect and serve?"

Callaway's face was stony, unrelenting. "We also swear to uphold the law."

"The law is there to work *for* justice, not to impede it."

He sighed, as if he would have preferred to agree with her. "I hear you. But many a tyrant has made the same argument you're making now. It's an imperfect system, but that doesn't mean the solution is to give people – you, me, anybody – the power to override it when we think we know better."

Harley fell silent. She understood his reasoning. After all, she had felt the very same way once upon a time. The first time she saw a killer go free on a technicality, however, her certainty about the merits of obeying the letter of the law had begun to erode.

"I know you don't always like the way I do things," she continued, choosing her words carefully. "You probably think I'm too impetuous."

He grunted. "And you think I'm too slow."

She sensed an opportunity and sat up straighter, determined to convince him. "But maybe that's what we need: a way to balance one another. It worked out on the last case, didn't it?"

Callaway stared through the windshield, his face half in shadow. He ran his knuckles slowly back and forth against the side of his jaw, a contemplative gesture that had become familiar to Harley.

"If my methods are a problem," Harley said, "I'll sit down with

Newbury. I'm sure there are other cases I could be working on."

She waited, watching him and hoping he would tell her this wasn't necessary. She wanted to hear that he valued her approach, that any concerns had been answered by her work on the Navarro case—a case Callaway very well might not have solved without her. And if she had colored outside the lines a time or two, what did that matter, given the results?

As always, the gears of Callaway's mind ground slowly.

"One step at a time," he finally answered. "The Kavers case is in the past. Just promise me that if you're going to try anything like that again, you'll run it by me first."

"You sure you don't want plausible deniability?"

"I want a chance to talk you down, not cover my ass."

Harley nodded, deciding she could respect that. "Deal." She put her hand out. Callaway gave her a long look as he shook her hand, as if not entirely sure what he was signing up for.

"Guess we're really partners now," Harley said as she sat back, relieved he had taken the news as well as he had. He could have gone straight to Newbury and demanded she be put on another case. He had seniority here, after all. Whatever trust and respect they had built together, she would have had to start the process over with someone else, just when she needed all the consistency she could get.

Her phone lit up, a beacon in the dark cabin. A text from Bryce Forrester, the high school sweetheart with whom she had briefly reconnected during the Navarro case.

Still moving into your new place tonight? I can swing by, help out

He was nothing if not determined. She smiled as she texted back: *Don't worry about it. Talk tomorrow.*

As she set her phone in the cup holder, she caught Callaway watching her, one eyebrow raised like an unspoken invitation.

"Just a friend offering to help me move my things," she explained, deciding there was no need to excavate the past with Callaway. "Mind dropping me off at the new place?"

Callaway nodded slowly. Harley had the impression his mind was still on the previous topic of their conversation, and she suspected he might be ruminating over it for a while.

"Want me to update the boss?" he said.

Harley considered, then shook her head. "No, I'll take care of it. My brain's still running too fast for sleep. The conversation might help me slow down a bit."

As they pulled out of the parking lot and headed toward Harley's new home, she said, "Did you really meet your wife at a kickboxing class?"

Callaway grinned. "She kicked my ass. That's how I knew she was the one."

*

Harley watched the taillights of Callaway's truck fade into the night, hoping she hadn't been foolish to trust him with so much information. Only time would tell. With an effort, she turned her attention to her new home.

The three-bedroom ranch-style house was by almost any definition a downgrade from the one she had shared with Rob. It was smaller (by about five hundred square feet), shorter (the Cape-style Massachusetts home had boasted a second story with four dormers), and surrounded by loose rock in place of grass, with a one-car garage and no backyard shed for Rob's hobby projects.

To Harley, however, it felt like a considerable upgrade. There was no lawn for her to maintain, less space for her to decorate and keep clean, and best of all privacy. Whereas in Massachusetts only a thin row of boxwoods had separated her from the neighbors only thirty feet away (close enough to hear their arguments, especially in the warmer months when the windows were open), this new house was guarded on three sides by a five-foot-high stone wall, beyond which stood miles and miles of open land occupied only by a herd of horses.

I could get used to the quiet here, she thought, pulling out her phone as she walked toward the front door, past the Jeep and U-Haul parked in the driveway. She called Newbury. She was opening the front door when Newbury answered, just before the call would have gone to voicemail.

"What can I do for you, Harley?" he said in a distracted voice. Harley could hear the chatter of voices in the background. "I'm at my son's Little League game."

"Just wanted to keep you up-to-date on the case," she answered, stepping into the house. The overhead light was already on. The officer who had returned her Jeep must have decided to take a look around and forgotten to turn it off.

"Have you spoken with your suspect yet?" Newbury said. The background conversations faded, suggesting Newbury had moved away from the crowd.

"He was meeting with a parole officer at the time of the killings," she explained, her voice loud in the empty house as she walked toward the kitchen.

Newbury cursed. "So where does that leave us?"

She stepped into the kitchen, deciding she could use a glass of water. She tested the filtered water feature on the front of the refrigerator. It looked clean enough.

"I'm thinking of heading back over to Holy Hope in the morning," she said, opening the cabinets in the hope that someone might have left a cup behind. She didn't want to go digging through the U-Haul just so she could get a drink of water.

"They should be a wellspring of information," she continued, "given what they knew of the victims, if I can get them to open up. They don't trust outsiders, especially federal agents."

She wanted to believe they treated all outsiders the same way, but she couldn't help feeling they maintained a special kind of distrust for her in particular, just like the glass blower at the farmers market. It didn't seem to matter that she'd spent the first eighteen years – just over half her life – in New Mexico. She had left, and because of that she was branded an outsider, or so it felt.

"They're cagey, sure," Newbury answered with a sympathetic sigh. "They think it's us against them. You need to find a way to establish trust."

Harley opened another set of cabinets. "Any suggestions on how to do that?"

Through the phone, Harley heard the sharp crack of a bat, followed by a loud cheer. Newbury was silent for several moments, but she could hear his breathing.

"Listen, I have to go," he finally said. "My advice? I've dealt with these people once or twice before, and they're naturally distrustful of strangers. But they used to have a good relationship with the police. One of their founding members was an ex-cop, so this whole distrust for authority goes only skin-deep. Bring them in on the investigation, share what you know, and you'll gain their trust."

The sounds from the ball game grew muffled. Then Harley heard Newbury shout something—it sounded like it might have been a few words of encouragement to his boy.

Then he was back on the phone again. "That's all I can say. My wife's already giving me the stink-eye, so I really have to go."

"I appreciate the help," Harley answered, not wishing to cause her boss any family problems. "I'll let you know how it goes."

"Please do that."

Harley hung up the phone. As she continued searching the cabinets, she mulled over Newbury's advice. It was strange, hearing him suggest she involve the members of Holy Hope in the investigation. Ordinarily, one of her highest responsibilities was to control the flow of information. The less the killer knew about the investigation, the better.

Then again, the investigation might not get far if nobody at Holy Hope would talk to her.

She opened another cupboard and discovered a pair of wine glasses. She froze. The logo on the side of the glasses was from a winery she had frequented in New England. These were *her* glasses, she realized. But who had gone through her things, and why had they placed the glasses here?

Just as she reached for one of the wine glasses, a loud thump came from another room. She stiffened.

Someone else was in the house.

CHAPTER TEN

Her heartbeat quickened as she scanned the kitchen for anything she might use as a weapon. It was bare, of course. Landlords were not known to leave complimentary blocks of knives.

Wishing once again she had her service weapon, she crept into the dining room. "Anyone there?" she called, supposing she had already made enough noise to alert anyone else in the house of her presence.

No answer came.

Creeping past the back entrance of the house, a sliding glass door that looked out on a columned patio, she noticed a truck she had never seen before parked beside the stone wall, the tailgate down. She could dimly see the outline of boxes in the back of the truck.

As she was puzzling over this, a hand touched her shoulder. She spun around, knocking the hand aside and raising her fists, her hundred hours of close-quarters training back at Quantico kicking in.

Her gaze fell on a tall, broad-shouldered man in his early thirties. He was handsome in a rugged, self-assured way, like a young Clint Eastwood.

The man took a step back, his eyes widening. "Woah, take it easy. I was just trying to help."

At the sight of her high school crush, the tension in Harley's body drained away, leaving her confused. "Bryce? What are you doing here? Didn't you hear me call out?"

Bryce pointed to the earbud still cradled in his ear. The second one rested in his palm.

"I know you said not to worry about it," he explained, "but I was up anyway with a pregnant broodmare, so I decided to come over and help you get a head start."

"And go through my things, too?" she said with a half-smile, feeling both bothered that he had taken such a liberty and pleased to see him.

He gave her that lazy, disarming smile she remembered so well, and shrugged. "I thought you'd appreciate the help. If you want me to go, though…"

He paused, letting the words linger. Harley, still battling contrary emotions, shook her head and smiled back. "Don't be ridiculous. I'm glad you came. You just scared the shit out of me, is all. Why didn't you park out front?"

"I had some things to bring around. Come on, take a look. I wanted to surprise you."

Still not entirely sure what to make of the unexpected visit, Harley followed Bryce down the hall to one of the bedrooms at the end, where he had set up her two bookshelves and filled them with books. He had even divided them into sections: psychology (perhaps the biggest section), criminology, biography, history, a smaller section of fiction. A desk and chair stood against the wall, a lamp casting a halo on the painted surface of the desk.

"The rest of the furniture is in the garage," Bryce explained, nudging an empty box aside with his foot. "I wasn't quite sure where you'd want things, and—well, I remember how opinionated you used to be."

"Can't say I've changed much," Harley murmured, only half-listening. Looking around the room, she felt a sudden burst of gratitude. Ever since Rob had surprised her with the news that he wanted a divorce, she had felt adrift, with no port to call home. Now, for the first time since then, she felt she had a safe place she could go at the end of a long day. No more sleeping in hotels, carting luggage around, worrying about where to forward her mail and which online accounts she needed to update.

She was back. She was home.

"So?" Bryce said, watching her. "What do you think?"

She smiled, overwhelmed by the gesture. "I think you're welcome to show up unannounced any time you want. This is great, Bryce. I'd offer you something to eat, but..."

He pressed a finger to her lips. "Hold that thought." His spurs gave a faint jingle as he stepped back into the hallway.

He stopped and turned back to face her. "Well?" he said, raising his eyebrows expectantly. "You coming?"

Puzzled, Harley followed him to the kitchen, where he gathered the two wine glasses she had discovered earlier.

"I still can't believe you went through my things," she said in good-natured disbelief.

He shrugged innocently. "It was for a good cause. I also took the liberty of getting you a little house-warming present." He opened the refrigerator and took out an unopened bottle of Merlot.

The sight of the familiar label sent a thrill of nostalgia through Harley. She stared at it, blinking in surprise. "Is that...?"

He nodded, smiling. "How old were we, fifteen? Sixteen?"

"You promised me your parents wouldn't even notice the difference. Then we drank almost the whole bottle."

Bryce chuckled as he pulled a corkscrew from the pocket of his jeans and began to drill into the cork. "Grounded me for two weeks— no TV, no Atari, and worst of all *no* Harley Cole."

"I was devastated," she murmured, watching him pull the cork free with an audible pop. "We were so close."

"Inseparable," he agreed. He filled the glasses and handed one to her. As their fingers touched, she suspected he was about to ask her the same question he had asked back then: Why did she have to leave?

To her relief, however, he merely shook his head with a sad smile. "We were just kids, playing at being adults."

He fell silent. Unsure what else to do, Harley swirled the cherry-red wine, closing her eyes as she inhaled. The scent was almost enough to bring her back to that golden time when she was still free to be a kid, when she still had two fun-loving siblings and a dad who liked to plan adventures with them on the weekends.

She opened her eyes to see Bryce staring at her with a mixture of amusement and fondness.

"To childhood," she said, raising her glass.

Resting his hand on her wrist, Bryce gently lowered her glass. "Not here. There's something you need to see."

"You're just full of intrigue tonight, aren't you?" she marveled.

He winked. "Haven't I always been?"

She followed Bryce through the house again, this time going out through the back door, which he held open for her. After she crossed the threshold, he turned off the lights.

Moving around his truck, Bryce set his glass on the stone wall. Harley did the same. Then, leaning his back against the wall, Bryce cupped his hands in front of his waist, making a sling as he had so many times before, back when they were two rambunctious, tree-climbing kids.

The memory sent a thrill of excitement through Harley. Without saying anything, she stepped into his hands and felt him lift her toward the wall. There was no tension in his face, no sign that he had any difficulty handling her.

I bet he'd make a good dancer, she thought, surprising herself. Bryce had, in fact, been a strikingly *bad* dancer: never quite sure how to follow the music, always stepping on Harley's toes.

But who knew how much might have changed since then?

As Harley made herself comfortable on the wall, Bryce rested his hands beside her. In the brief moment before he pulled himself up, she noticed a faint circlet of bleached skin on his ring finger, the striking absence of a wedding ring.

He had been wearing a ring when she bumped into him just before the start of the Navarro case. Had his world changed as much as hers in the past month?

"Well, this is nice," she said, kicking her feet the way she used to when she was little. A bat darted along the roof of the house. Above the chorus of crickets, coyotes called to one another in the distance, a sound that had once frightened Harley but now felt comforting. The air tasted dry and sweet.

"And you haven't even noticed the best part yet," Bryce answered. He pointed up. Harley tilted her head back at the vast expanse of stars spread over them. She took a sharp breath.

"I could never see the stars like this in the city," she said, moved by the sight. "Even on clear nights."

"Feels good, don't it?"

She lay back, knees raised, while Bryce watched her with a gentle smile. She closed her eyes, enjoying the coolness of the stones beneath her.

A pleasant silence stretched between them. Finally Harley sat up, remembering the wine. She picked up her glass. "So, what shall we toast?"

"Your new home, of course," Bryce answered, picking up his own glass. "May it be everything you're looking for."

She smiled, clinked her glass against his, and took a swallow. It tasted of black cherries and chocolate, but her mind wasn't really on the taste. She was thinking of Bryce's words. Was he talking only of the house, or of himself as well?

Feeling a bit uncomfortable at the way he was studying her, she decided to turn the attention on him. "So how have the years treated you? Did you ever settle down?"

He stared into his glass, growing contemplative. "In a manner of speaking, I guess. I thought for sure I'd get out of here, just like you did, but then my dad injured his leg in a riding accident. Couldn't keep track of the ranch by himself, so I stayed on."

He paused to take another swallow.

"He passed some years back—congestive heart failure. Mom went not long after."

Harley touched his knee. "I'm so sorry, Bryce."

He nodded. "I was with Josie by then, and I thought we'd run the ranch together." He laughed and shook his head. "You know what they say about best-laid plans."

Harley sat up, alert. "You don't mean Josie Roche, do you?" Josie Roche had been Harley's best friend throughout most of her childhood. It gave Harley a queasy feeling, imagining them together.

Bryce nodded ruefully, as if he should have known better. "You had that going-away party at Josie's place, remember?"

Harley thought back across the years. Yes, she remembered the party, and she remembered Bryce had surprised her by coming. Had she invited him? She didn't remember.

"After you left," he continued, "I stuck around to help Josie pick up before her parents got home. I guess I'd given up on convincing you to stay—you were hellbent on going."

"I remember." She watched him, trying to decide whether he still held her decision against her. It was clear he still felt the rejection of her choice, but the fact that he had shown up to help her move in – when she had told him not to worry about it, no less – suggested he wasn't holding a grudge.

He drained the rest of his wine, set the glass aside, and leaned back on his palms. "I don't think I really need to explain the rest. Josie and I were both devastated about losing you, and I don't think either of us really understood why you were leaving. So we had that in common."

I brought them together, Harley thought, searching her heart for jealousy at this revelation. She felt only curiosity, however—that and a pang of longing for how things might have gone differently if she had stayed.

"I had to go," she said, wanting him to understand. "After Kelly disappeared, and then the way my dad changed—"

Bryce held up a hand to stop her. "I know, I know. I think I get it now. I wasn't trying to make you feel guilty."

She waited for him to continue.

"Anyway," he went on, "Josie and I gave it a try, and it worked for a while, but eventually our luck ran out. She's back with her folks now. We've been separated for about two years, but now we're making it official."

Harley felt a sudden kinship toward this man she had once loved. What would her life have been like if she had stayed? Would they have married, enjoyed a fairytale romance together?

"I'm sorry," she murmured. "It's not easy—I know from experience."

He studied her with sad, solemn eyes. She suspected he was waiting for her to open up about her own marriage, but she wasn't ready to do so. She wasn't ready to be that vulnerable that quickly.

"Any kids?" she said, shifting the focus back on him again.

"Jadon," Bryce answered. "He's six now. He comes to the ranch now and then—a few weekends a month, usually."

Harley absorbed this, wondering if she would have been in the same situation if she'd agreed to have kids with Rob instead of prioritizing her career.

They both fell silent. Harley sensed that if they stayed there much longer, she would either fall asleep or she and Bryce would do something they might later regret. She enjoyed his company, but the truth was that, despite their shared history, they hardly knew one another. She didn't need to complicate her life further by jumping into the deep end of a relationship.

She stifled a yawn. "This was nice, Bryce. Really, I appreciate you helping me get settled in. I'd love to keep talking, but it's been a long day and I need to be up early tomorrow."

Bryce sat up, nodding. "Of course."

Harley sensed a trace of disappointment in his voice. Before she could decide how to respond, however, he smiled.

"Wouldn't want to stop you from catching killers."

He dropped down to the ground, then looked up at her. "You want any help setting up the rest of your furniture, just let me know, okay?"

"Don't your horses need you?"

"Doesn't mean I can't steal a few hours away for an old friend."

Harley smiled as Bryce tipped his hat and moved toward his truck.

As the rumble of the truck's engine faded into the night, exhaustion settled on Harley like a weighted blanket. Retrieving a set of bedding from the garage, she spread it on the couch and collapsed on it. She could make her bed tomorrow night. In the meantime, the couch would do.

As she drifted off to sleep, she thought about Bryce's words. *Is that what I am to him?* she wondered. *An old friend?*

CHAPTER ELEVEN

Something was buzzing in the room.

Harley shifted groggily, thinking some kind of large insect must have gotten trapped in the room—a cicada, maybe, or one of those stink bugs that sounded so much like a WWII bomber.

As she eased open her sleep-crusted eyes, however, she saw her phone glowing on her discarded pair of pants. She picked it up and swiped to the right to receive the call, clearing her throat as she did so.

The voice of Sheriff Santiago crackled in her ear.

"Morning, Harley. Sorry to call so early, but we have a situation on our hands."

Harley scooted back and slipped her feet to the floor, forcing her mind to focus on the case. "Did you find another body?"

"No, thank God, it's not that," he answered, and Harley heard a papery rattle, like blinds being bent. "Not yet, anyway."

Harley held the phone between her head and shoulder while pulling up her pants. "Not yet?" she repeated, puzzled by the sheriff's cryptic answer.

"Some people have marched down from Holy Hope," he continued, sounding troubled. "They're claiming two of their teenage members have gone missing."

Harley stopped buttoning her pants. "Wait, two *more* of their members?"

"That's what they claim. Look, just get down here soon as you can, alright? I'll keep them calm long as I can, but you know more about this case than I do."

"What are you expecting me to tell them?"

"They need hope, Harley. They need to know the killer can't just run amok, doing as he pleases."

That's exactly what he's doing, Harley thought, but she knew better than to say it. She took a deep breath and let it out slowly.

"Okay," she said. "Keep them occupied. I'll be there as soon as I can."

"Thanks, Harley. See you soon."

As Harley hung up the phone, she wondered at the note of relief she'd heard in the sheriff's voice. Couldn't he just take a few statements and then send them home? How much trouble could a bunch of off-gridders really cause?

The bigger question, however, was about the disappearances themselves. Had the killer struck again? And if so, how long would it be before the bodies showed up?

*

As Harley neared the Huerta County Sheriff's Department, she needed only one glance at the angry mob gathered by the front doors to understand the sheriff's reaction. There must have been thirty or forty people in all, both men and women, grumbling to one another or casting a few choice words in the direction of the pair of deputies guarding the building's entrance.

That's why he sounded so rattled, Harley thought. *He's in over his head.*

She had called Callaway on the drive over and filled him in. He had already been up, checking out the house where Sienna and Eleanor had lived just outside Holy Hope. He hadn't found anything of note.

A number of heads turned to squint at the Jeep as Harley parked, though the glare of early morning sunlight on the windshield must have made it impossible for them to see through. She stepped out, straightening her back and tucking a lock of hair behind her ear.

"What seems to be the problem?" she said as she neared the mob.

"The fact that our people are dying and you're doing nothing about it!" someone shouted. "How's that for starters?" There were resentful murmurs of agreement.

So much for wanting nothing to do with law enforcement, Harley thought. Something truly terrible must have happened to send them running to the police.

"I promise you," she answered, keeping a calm and professional demeanor, "we're doing everything we can to—"

"Well, that's not good enough! How are we supposed to feel safe, knowing there's a killer on the loose and you're dragging your feet?"

Harley was about to explain that she was not, in fact, dragging her feet, when the front door opened and Sheriff Santiago's face appeared. "Agent Cole, why don't you come on in?"

The mob fell silent as Harley moved past them, slipping between the pair of deputies before entering the building. It was dark inside. Her eyes were still adjusting to the change when she felt the sheriff's hand on her shoulder.

"Thank you for coming, Agent Cole," he said in a solemn tone. "This is Melissa Hargrave, one of the founders of Holy Hope. She's here as a spokesman—spokes*woman* of sorts." He cleared his throat as if to smooth over the mistake.

"Yes, we've met," Harley replied, studying the older woman. Her gray-and-white hair was pulled back in a ponytail so tight that it looked like her scalp might tear free any minute. Her gaze was frosty as she stared at Harley.

"You didn't tell us we were being stalked like deer," she said stiffly. "How are any of us supposed to go back to our lives, wondering who'll be taken next?"

Harley glanced at Santiago, whose eyebrows were raised as he watched her in expectant silence. It seemed as if both of them were expecting Harley to have all the answers, maybe tell them she had already identified the killer-turned-kidnapper and had a team of agents on their way to arrest him as they spoke. If only the truth were so glamorous.

"Let's back up a bit," she said. "Tell me about these kidnappings."

Gardenia snorted and shook her head. "Why should I tell you anything? Sienna and Eleanor are already dead, and you've done nothing to catch the killer. Excuse me if I don't have much confidence you'll be able to help."

"It's been one day," Harley answered, holding up both hands in a calming gesture. "We promise we're doing everything we can, but it may take some time."

"And what are we supposed to do in the meantime? Hide in our homes and lock our doors? Pray the vengeful angel passes on?"

"If you have reason to believe your lives are in danger—"

"We need to arm ourselves, that's what we need to do," Gardenia continued, her voice bitter as she paced across the carpeted floor. "If you can't protect us, we'll just have to police ourselves."

Harley felt Santiago's eyes on her, pleading with her to get a handle on the situation. If Gardenia was serious, and if the people of Holy Hope began stockpiling weapons to defend themselves, there was no telling what might happen. Fear had a way of making people trigger-happy.

Newbury's advice from the previous night came back to her.

"Look," she began in a conciliatory tone, "I know you don't trust us. You figure that because you've got your own separate community and don't do things the way the rest of us do, we don't care what happens to you."

Gardenia stopped pacing and crossed her arms, staring at Harley as if to say, *Are we wrong?*

"But here's the problem," Harley continued. "You won't help us until we prove you wrong, but we might not be able to prove you wrong — by catching the killer, I mean — without your help. Catch-22."

"So what do you suggest?"

Harley felt Santiago's eyes on her. "Collaboration," she answered. "We share information with you, you share information with us."

Gardenia's eyebrows shot up in exaggerated disbelief. "You want me to be a mole? Give you the inside scoop about what's going on at Holy Hope?"

"And in return, I'll keep you posted on the investigation. If there's a dangerous character you need to watch out for, you'll be the first to know."

She paused, half expecting Santiago to protest. There was no telling what Gardenia might do with the information Harley gave her, nor how far it might spread. Santiago, however, remained silent.

Gardenia stared hard at Harley for a few moments before nodding. "Fine. But it's a two-way street, remember. Don't come to me for information if you're not willing to share anything in return."

Harley nodded back. "Fair enough."

"So what do you know?"

Harley hesitated. "Before we get started, we need to lay some ground rules. Anything we tell you must be kept in the strictest of confidence. You can't share it with your friends, your family, the media. It stays between us. Anything else could jeopardize the investigation."

Gardenia shrugged, as if this were a small concession. "Okay. I can live with that." She looked around until she spotted a wooden chair, then she sank down into it, perching on the edge of the seat. "Tell me about Gale Underwood. Is he still in custody?"

Harley pulled out a chair for herself and sat down opposite Gardenia. Santiago looked on, occasionally moving to the window to cast a worried eye on the crowd gathered there.

Gardenia's knowledge of Gale's arrest surprised Harley. "How did you—" Harley began, but the older woman cut her off.

"Oh, please. With the scene you made at the market? How could I *not* know about it?" She leaned forward intently. "So why don't you think he committed the murders?"

"He has an alibi—a good one."

Gardenia leaned back and shrugged, as if this didn't really surprise her. "It's just as well. If he's still locked up, he couldn't have anything to do with the disappearances, and even though I want to believe those two girls just got lost on a hike…" Lines of worry creased her forehead.

"Anyway," she went on, "it seems like quite the coincidence."

Harley sat up straighter, pleased Gardenia had brought up the disappearances. She pulled out her phone to take notes. "Who went missing?"

Gardenia hesitated as if it caused her physical pain to volunteer the information. "Isla Clemente and Beverly Morris. Isla's fifteen, Bev's seventeen. They're good friends."

Another pair, Harley mused, though they were younger than the first two victims, who had both been in their forties. "When did they go missing?"

"Bev was supposed to haul water for the gardens this morning—fill a big washtub from the well, then I dunk my watering can in it. She does it every morning like clockwork, so when I found the tub empty this morning, I started asking around. Nobody had seen her since last night."

"Sure she didn't go into town?"

Gardenia shook her head, dismissing the idea. "She knew her responsibilities, and she liked the routine. It calmed her. Besides, all the vehicles were accounted for."

"What about hitchhiking?"

Gardenia snorted. "Bev is just about as shy as they come. She'd never get into a vehicle with a stranger, especially not a man."

This caught Harley's attention. She paused, looking up from her phone. "Especially not a man?"

"She never told me about it, but you could tell she went through a lot before she came here. It's not uncommon. Most of the young women at Holy Hope come there to escape some kind of abuse."

Harley noted this. "And the other girl?" she said. "Isla?"

"Like I said, the two of them are good friends. Thick as thieves. As soon as we found Bev was missing, it was only natural to search for Isla. When nobody could recall seeing them since last night, we knew we had a problem on our hands."

"Can you think of anyone who might have wanted to harm them? Anyone in the community who might have suspicious motives?"

Gardenia arched an eyebrow. "We're a generally welcoming community, but we don't harbor sexual predators, if that's what you're getting at."

You harbored Underwood, Harley thought. It caused her to wonder who else in Holy Hope might be using a false name to escape their past sins.

"Ms. Hargrave," she began, "I know you don't care for outsiders, least of all when they're sent by the government. But I'm doing everything in my power to solve this case, and I need your full cooperation. If there's anything you can tell me, even the smallest detail that seems the least bit suspicious..."

A light came on in Gardenia's eyes. She squinted thoughtfully, nodding.

"Now that you mention it," she said, "there is someone worth looking into. I didn't think of him before because he left the community about a month ago."

"Name?"

"Hector Nunez."

Harley glanced at Santiago, wondering if she should recognize the name.

"I've run into him a time or two," the sheriff admitted. "Petty drug dealer."

"Wish I'd known that before he joined our community," Gardenia muttered. "We kicked him out for trying to recruit some of our younger members to sell drugs in town."

"Pot?" Harley said. Recreational marijuana had recently become legal in the state, but it still carried a taboo in some areas.

Gardenia shook her head. "Try meth. Now that I think about it, Bev was the one who turned him in—said she'd seen him following Isla around, and she was afraid Isla was going to get involved."

"Did you call the police?"

Gardenia snorted. "For what? We told him to pack his things and get out. Believe it or not, we do a pretty good job handling our own problems."

The air stirred as the front door opened. Harley glanced over to see Callaway striding in, folding his sunglasses and slipping them into the breast pocket of his dress shirt.

Harley rose. "Thank you for your time, Ms. Hargrave. If you think of anything else, you know how to reach us."

"Just remember your promise," Gardenia answered. "If you come in with the cavalry to arrest one of my people, and you don't warn me in advance, there'll be hell to pay."

Harley watched the woman rise and leave the building. She had no doubt Gardenia meant every word.

Outside, Harley could see Gardenia speaking to the crowd of Holy Hopers. After a few moments, the crowd moved away from the building, gathered around Gardenia like children around a magician.

"What'd I miss?" Callaway said, looking back and forth between Harley and Santiago.

Harley sighed with relief as she ran a hand over her face. "We've got two missing girls, teenagers," she explained. "Gardenia mentioned an ex-member by the name of Hector Nunez—some kind of drug dealer who was thrown out of the community about a month ago."

"Deals out of an old ghost town," Santiago added. "It's like a drive-through for drugs."

"If you know what he's doing," Harley answered, "why haven't you busted him?"

Santiago gave a mirthless chuckle. "I don't have the manpower to root out every drug dealer, shoplifter, and arsonist in the county. Besides, if I lock him up, someone will spring up in his place within twenty-four hours. Just the nature of the beast."

"What's the name of the place?" Callaway said.

"*Los Muertos Afortunados.*"

"The Lucky Dead," Harley mused.

Santiago nodded. "Was built during the first gold rush in the early 1800s. Plenty of people got rich overnight. Then the cholera epidemic of 1833 hit, wiping out most of the town. That's how the town got its name—nobody remembers what it was before that."

"Can't imagine why nobody would want to live there now," Callaway said dryly.

"Nobody except Nunez and a few customers with nowhere better to go," the sheriff answered.

Harley offered her hand to Santiago. "As always, thank you for your help," she said.

As they shook hands, however, she remembered the voicemail Santiago had left about Kelly. She wanted more than anything to ask him what he had found. But considering how recently the two teenage girls had gone missing, she knew she did not have a moment to spare.

Santiago seemed to understand what she was thinking. He smiled gently. "We'll talk again soon, Harley. It can wait."

It's been waiting eighteen years, she thought disconsolately, but she knew he was right. It could wait a little longer.

As the two agents headed for the doors, Harley said to Callaway, "When Underwood mentioned partying with Sienna and Eleanor, did he say anything about drugs?"

Callaway held the door open for her. "Jacob Boudoin, you mean? No, I don't think so. Looking for anything particular?"

"Methamphetamines."

"Think there's a connection here with Nunez?"

"Worth looking into. It's not like we can sit on our hands for a month while we wait for the toxicology report."

"Even if they did get methamphetamines from Nunez," Callaway said, "you really think Boudoin will just volunteer a confession to a federal crime?"

Harley smiled. "Use some of that folksy Southern charm you have in such abundance. If it's an opportunity for him to escape the assault charge, he'll talk."

As they entered the parking lot, Callaway suddenly stopped in his tracks.

"Oh," he said, "I almost forgot something."

He opened the passenger door of his truck and leaned in. Unlatching the dashboard compartment, Callaway pulled out a gold badge, a holstered Glock 19 with two spare magazines, and a pair of shiny new handcuffs.

"Figured it was about time you got these back," he said, handing them to Harley.

Harley hadn't realized how much she missed the tools of her trade until she held them in her hands again. She nodded gratefully. "You have no idea. It's like being a Rottweiler with no teeth. What's the point?"

As she walked to her Jeep so she could follow Callaway to *Los Muertos Afortunados,* she realized this was her first official day on the job in a long time. It was a good feeling, after how things had unraveled since the conclusion of the Kavers case.

She followed Callaway through town and then out into the desert, enjoying the familiar feel of the holster against her hip. It was time to catch a killer.

CHAPTER TWELVE

Harley stretched her arm out of the Jeep's window and pointed at a row of mesquites beside the road, gesturing for Callaway to pull over. They had almost passed the trees – there was nothing for cover beyond them but the occasional cholla cactus, which stood no chance of disguising the vehicles – when the brake lights of the truck lit up as Callaway turned off the road.

"What's the holdup?" he said as he joined Harley between the two vehicles. The early sun was still climbing, casting slanting rays that drew long shadows among the mesquites. Despite how young the day was, however, heat rose in shimmering waves off the roofs of the vehicles.

Harley studied the ghost town about a quarter mile away. Los Muertos Afortunados was even smaller than she had expected, no more than a scattering of ramshackle buildings flanking an unmarked dirt road in the middle of miles of barren grassland. A few vehicles passed through, but otherwise there were no signs of life.

"If we get any closer," she said, "he'll spot us for sure."

Callaway looked offended. "What, you don't think Feds like to have a good time now and then?"

She raised an eyebrow. "That's your cover? Show him your badge and then reassure him you're off the clock?"

"I'll make up a story. Something will come to me—it always does."

Harley was not sure whether to be annoyed by his confidence or envious of it. Normally he was the one who preferred to have all the details planned in advance, and she was the one ready to wing it. Now their roles were reversed.

"If you drive up there and spook him," she answered, "he's going to run, whether or not he has anything to do with the murders."

Callaway shrugged as if this were a minor detail. "So we trap him—the old pincer movement. I'll drive all the way around to the other side of the town, and when you see me approaching, you enter from this side. He'll have nowhere to run."

Harley was still considering the plan when her phone rang. She hesitated, staring at the name: JOHN COLE. She wanted to believe her hesitation was about the investigation: It was conceivable Nunez might

70

glimpse the flash of sunlight off their vehicles even through the trees, and he might run. This wasn't the time for a personal call.

But that's not really the problem, is it? she thought. No. The real problem was that her last few conversations with her father had gone remarkably well, and she sensed it could only go downhill from there.

Callaway sidled closer and read the name on the phone. When he saw it, he pressed his lips together in a sympathetic expression.

"Go on," he urged gently. "You can spare a few minutes for your dying father."

Taking a calming breath, Harley answered the phone. "Hey, Dad. Everything alright?"

"Sure, yeah, everything's great. Just checking in to see how my little girl's doing." There was a note of levity that rang false to Harley's ears, like he was trying too hard to connect with the daughter he had seen so little of throughout her adult life.

"You get moved into your new place yet?" he added.

"Yeah—somewhat, I mean. Bryce helped me last night."

Callaway raised an eyebrow at this. Harley turned away, not wanting him to read her face.

"Bryce Forrester?" her father said, sounding amazed. "I haven't seen him in years. He still around?"

"Still around."

"You two have a chance to catch up? Mend fences, so to speak?"

She knew what he was angling for. He wanted her to settle down, just as he had wanted her to settle with Rob. She had only recently told her father about the divorce, and he had responded surprisingly well. Perhaps he supposed losing his son-in-law was the requisite sacrifice for regaining his daughter.

"Listen, Dad, I'm in the middle of something and can't really talk now. But we're still on for lunch tomorrow, right?"

A pause. When her father spoke again, his voice was different—reluctant, as if he had bad news to share.

"About that. We're going to have to reschedule. These meds they've got me on really wreak havoc on my system. Can't stomach much more than soup and crackers." He uttered a dry, hollow chuckle.

"Soup and crackers, then," she suggested, turning as a metallic jingle caught her attention. Callaway was dangling his keys at her as he opened the door of his truck, letting her know he was going to drive around to the other side of the town.

"We'll pretend we're eating out," she continued, nodding at Callaway to say she understood. "Just like when we were kids, and

71

Mom would make menus for us. Do you remember that?"

She waited, watching as Callaway pulled back onto the road and made a U-turn.

"No, I wouldn't want to impose," her father answered with a politeness that sounded forced. "You've got a new case you're working, a house to move into, old friends to catch up with. Your hands are full. We can talk another time, when you're not so busy."

Even after all these years, she thought with amazement, *he's still punishing me for leaving.*

She decided to offer one more olive branch.

"What time, then?" she said. "Let's plan a day."

Another long silence.

"We'll see how I'm feeling in the next few days," he replied, "once I get used to this new medication. I'll let you know."

How could he spend years guilting her for leaving, and then avoid her when she came back? Did he prefer thinking of himself as a victim—the poor widower who lost both his daughters, one by a mysterious tragedy and the other by willful neglect?

"Okay," she answered, biting back the angry words her father could so easily incite. "Just let me know."

"Will do, sweetheart."

She winced at the term of endearment. It was a throwaway word, devoid of any genuine affection.

"I love you, Dad."

"You, too. Buh-bye."

She hung up the phone and shook her head, feeling her self-control slip away. Why was it that the people you loved most could also hurt you the most?

She caught a flash of metal in the distance and looked up to see Callaway's truck slowly approaching town from the opposite direction. She got into her Jeep, pulled back onto the road, and headed toward Los Muertos Afortunados, shoving aside all thoughts of her father as she focused her attention back on the case.

She passed an ancient-looking Cadillac buried in dirt up to the running boards, a perfect symbol of the town's bygone wealth. Beyond that was the remains of a church: three walls of cemented stone, with a row of windows revealing a grassy sanctuary. Closer to the center of town stood a cluster of rundown buildings, the wood gray and warped by the sun, along with a single adobe building that seemed to have withstood the test of time.

A Lincoln town car with tinted windows stopped beside the adobe building. Harley slowed, watching as the door to the house opened and a squat, bow-legged man in patched jeans stepped out, casting a practiced glance both ways while hardly moving his head. He was bald, and the sweat on his forehead gave off an angry gleam.

Hello, Hector Nunez, Harley thought.

The man she took to be Nunez leaned into the vehicle. A few moments later the car pulled away, and Nunez was looking around, his right hand coming empty out of his pocket. He saw Harley's vehicle and froze.

Easy, Hector. I'm just another customer.

She pulled forward, hoping to sell the act as long as possible. She wondered if he could see her through the windshield, and if so, what he saw. A thirty-something woman with auburn hair, wearing a V-neck blouse with the sleeves rolled back to the elbows? A bored mom looking to have a fun weekend away with the girlfriends?

Whatever Nunez did or did not see, he made a small gesture with his hand, lowering the palm and cutting his fingers sideways through the air. Stop? Wait? Harley was not sure how to take it. She watched him stroll back to the building, hoping he was just going back inside to retrieve another gram.

Seconds after the door closed, Callaway called.

"Think he's coming back out?" Callaway said.

"What choice does he have? He's trapped." Even as she said the words, though, she felt a shiver of uncertainty. Had they overlooked something? The last case she had worked, the Felix Navarro case, had involved a large compound built on a network of old mines. The killer had been using the tunnels to spirit his victims away from the property before leaving them to die in other tunnels far away.

Was it possible Nunez had a similar escape route?

"So, how long do you want to give him?" Callaway said. Harley could hear the uneasiness in his voice, as well. Something wasn't right here, and she wasn't going to sit on her hands and wait to find out what was going on.

"None," she replied, releasing her seatbelt. "I'm going in."

To her surprise, Callaway made no effort to slow her down. All he said was, "I'm right behind you," and then hung up.

Harley tried to move casually as she approached the building. She glanced to her right to see Callaway pulling up, and as she did so she noticed the figure at the corner of the building across from her. The building was the collapsed remains of a bank, judging by the sign, and the figure – man or woman, Harley could not tell – had long, greasy hair and wore what looked to be a dirty pink leotard. He or she grinned, made a pistol with the fingers of the left hand, and fired at Harley.

Harley tried to put this sinister gesture out of mind as she scanned the windows of the building. She thought she glimpsed the stirring of a curtain, but she could not be sure.

Then Callaway was beside her, casting a nonchalant glance up and down the street as Harley knocked on the door.

"Hector Nunez?" she called. "This is the FBI! We just want to talk!"

No answer. From across the road came a dry cackle.

"Can't say we didn't ask nicely," Callaway murmured. "Who's taking point?"

"I've got it," Harley answered, drawing her Glock. The weight felt good in her hands.

Harley stepped aside, watching as Callaway leaned back and kicked the door, shattering the wood around the lock. While the door was still swinging open, Harley rushed into the building.

"FBI!" she shouted. "Come out with your hands up!"

After the brightness of the morning, the interior of the building was a series of dim shapes, mere outlines of furniture, cardboard boxes, folding chairs. Crumpled tissues bloomed on the floor like fungus after a rain.

Her hip bumped a takeout carton, and a swarm of flies swirled past her face.

She cursed, ducking away from the flies as she moved into the kitchen, where a stack of dishes rose from the sink like a Jenga tower ready to topple. Something slipped beneath her shoe, and she glanced down to see a used condom smeared across the linoleum. She fought a sudden, overpowering urge to gag.

"Kitchen's clear!" she shouted.

"Dining room's clear!" Callaway echoed back. "Bathroom, too!"

Retracing her steps, she met up with Callaway and pushed toward the back of the house, where a single room remained, the door closed. Harley grasped the door and found it unlocked.

She glanced at Callaway, waited for him to nod back, then – in one smooth motion – she pulled the door open and stepped aside, allowing Callaway to advance into the room. She followed seconds later.

The bed was an air mattress, wrinkled from deflation and covered by a faded sheet that had popped off one of the corners of the bed. There was an exercise bike covered with a fine film of dust, an open window, and no Hector Nunez.

"Damn it!" Harley exclaimed, moving toward the window.

Before she could reach it, however, she heard a loud pop and ducked, instinctively pressing her back against the wall for cover. The adobe would stop most small caliber rounds, but if Nunez opened up with anything too large (a 7.62 millimeter AK-47, for instance), there was no telling whether the wall would hold. Harley hoped she would not have to find out.

As she waited to learn whether Nunez would fire again, she heard the rev of an engine.

"Wait a minute," Callaway said, frowning as he rose. "That was a backfire, not a gunshot."

Harley joined Callaway at the window. She looked out just in time to see Hector Nunez driving away in a Durango with a suspension lift, a cloud of dust pluming behind him.

"Come on!" Callaway said, grabbing her arm. "We'll take my truck—it's just out front."

CHAPTER THIRTEEN

"I should have taken my car," Harley said, planting one hand on the ceiling to keep herself in her seat. With every bump, the old truck tried to vomit her out the windshield, as if she were a bad meal it just didn't want to digest.

Callaway, however, seemed to be enjoying the adventure. He rode the bumps like a surfer, occasionally taking one hand off the wheel to adjust his hat.

"You just bought yours," he answered. "You gotta build trust before you try something like this."

Harley heard the lightness in his voice. It was relief, she realized. He liked the open chase, the sprint—not sneaking around in the darkness, waiting to see the flash of the muzzle that would end his life.

Harley could not blame him. Still, she wondered if he might be enjoying it a bit *too* much.

"Are you sure this old fossil can handle this?" she wondered aloud as they bounced over a large stone that would have tossed Harley into Callaway's lap, if not for the seat belt.

Callaway grinned at her. "She's never failed me before."

Ahead of them, tires kicking up a cloud of dirt and stone, Nunez climbed toward a sandstone bluff weathered by years of the desert wind's harsh treatment. The earth made a natural ramp up to the bluff.

"He's going to jump it," Harley murmured in disbelief.

Callaway said nothing. His mouth was set in a grim, determined line.

As they raced ever upward, nearing the bluff, Harley realized they were too late to stop Nunez. If he was going to make the jump, there was nothing they could do.

"We have to go around," she said. "Meet him at the bottom."

Callaway shook his head. "We'll lose too much time. He'll get away."

A chill went through her as she stared at Callaway. In a flash of insight, it occurred to her that her life was entirely in his hands. At this speed, bouncing over every dip and crease in the hills, one wrong move could send them rolling end-over-end, which would not only allow Nunez to escape but might also put both agents in the hospital. That was dangerous enough.

But to drive over the bluff, with no knowledge of what was on the other side?

"You're not seriously thinking of following him over, are you?" she said, thinking surely he was joking, surely the cool, level-headed Anthony Callaway wouldn't risk their lives in such a reckless gamble.

He faced her, his green eyes alive in a way Harley had rarely seen.

"Do you trust me?" he said.

Her response was automatic. "Of course I trust you."

"No. Do you *trust* me?"

The bluff approached. Already she could feel the dirt beneath the tires turn to stone. They were rapidly nearing the point at which it would be impossible for them to turn back.

In those few moments, she thought back to the rattlesnake she had accidentally disturbed in the mine while working the Navarro case, and the way Callaway had stepped in without hesitation to save her. She thought of the calming presence he had been beside her throughout that case. He didn't gamble, not unless the odds were heavily in his favor.

And he didn't act without some semblance of a plan, even when he was winging it.

"I really need to hear it, Harley!" Callaway shouted above the growl of the engine, above the rattle of stones in the tire wells. The veins on his hands stood out as he gripped the steering wheel.

"Yes, I trust you!" she answered, hoping she would not regret the words.

Callaway nodded slowly, his face relaxing as his breathing deepened. "I was hoping you'd say that. Hold on—this is about to get interesting."

That's a bit of an understatement, Harley thought.

The bluff rushed toward them. The horizon opened up, then a valley peppered with green plant life and boulders.

"Hold on!" Callaway shouted.

Harley held on as best she could. It reminded her of the time she had gone whitewater rafting with Rob, clinging to the raft for dear life as they navigated the hostile river.

What was decidedly different, however, was the sense of weightlessness that seemed to last an eternity as they soared through the air. Harley found herself trying to think if there was anything she should do. Her mind was clear, and there seemed to be plenty of time, but she couldn't think of anything to do with it.

Then the ground came up and slammed against them. There was a loud, grating sound as the truck spun, kicking up stones. As they slid sideways down the hill, Harley looked over to see Callaway staring through the windshield, his face scrunched as if waiting for impact.

The impact, however, never came. They slowed to a stop, the world ceased spinning, and – most miraculous of all – they were both alive and uninjured.

The same could not be said for Nunez, however. Glancing out the window, Harley saw his vehicle tumbling sideways down the slope. It made three or four revolutions before striking a stony outcropping.

Harley opened her door and jumped out. She felt unsteady for a moment (her heart had somehow climbed into her head, and the pressure was threatening to burst her ears), but then the world settled and she found her balance again.

Nunez's car lay on its back, a thin wisp of smoke curling up from the engine, which was still running. A blood-smeared hand reached out through the open window on the driver's side.

"Show me your other hand!" Harley ordered, aiming her gun at the shape crumpled in the vehicle.

Next came Nunez's bald head, which was already bruising. He slithered out like a calf escaping a dying cow. Harley finally saw his right hand pressed tight to his ribs, empty.

"Are you armed?" Harley said, not ready to lower her guard just yet.

Nunez shook his head. Just to be sure, Harley stepped forward and, after cuffing him, frisked him as well. She found only a pocket knife, which she tossed aside. Then, keeping an eye on Nunez to make sure he didn't get up, she reached into the vehicle and turned off the engine.

"Ambulance is on the way," Callaway, slipping his phone into his pocket as he caught up with them.

Nunez coughed, then winced as he clutched his side. "Some ride, wasn't it?"

Harley shook her head in disbelief. "Why'd you run, Hector?"

He tried to clear his throat and grimaced in pain. "Man, I ain't got to tell you shit."

Callaway raised his eyebrows. "No? You expect us to think you were just handing out candy back there? It's a little early for trick-or-treat."

Nunez said nothing. It occurred to Harley that they needed leverage, some way of *making* Nunez talk—particularly before the ambulance arrived. They had him cornered and caught off-guard right now. They couldn't give him time to invent a story, assuming he hadn't already done so.

Harley met Callaway's eyes and made a small gesture with her head toward Nunez's vehicle. Callaway nodded, understanding. Harley began feeling around the vehicle's wheel wells.

Callaway squatted down beside Nunez. "We can play hard ball if that's what you want. We'll go back to your place, tear it apart until we find your stash."

Nunez snorted. "Good luck to you."

This answer only reinforced Harley's suspicion that Nunez's drugs were in the car. She didn't think he would risk leaving them behind if he had to leave town in a hurry, as he had been trying to do just minutes earlier. The question was simply *where*.

"Okay," Callaway answered, rising. "No problem. We have all the time in the world."

Harley popped the gas cover open and began searching inside. Nunez heard the sound and turned his head, suddenly noticing what she was doing. His face twisted in anger.

"Hey, you can't do that! That's my car!"

"Probable cause," Callaway answered cheerfully. "Besides, you don't have anything to hide, right?"

Harley opened the back door and leaned into the vehicle.

"This is bullshit," Nunez was saying. "I didn't do anything wrong." A new thought seemed to occur to him. "Wait a minute, you're not cops. You're Feds."

"Winner winner, chicken dinner," Callaway said. "What gave us away? Was it the lack of uniforms?"

Harley began feeling the edges of the ceiling lining for any bumps where drugs might have been slipped in. It could take hours to thoroughly search a vehicle for drugs, but she didn't have that kind of time. She needed results before the ambulance arrived. In her experience, it didn't take long for career criminals to recover their poise.

"You're not just looking for drugs, are you?" Nunez said in a low voice.

"That depends," Callaway replied. "Is there another crime we should be aware of?"

Harley reached between the cushions of the seats suspended overhead. She found nothing but a soda cap and a few French fries that disintegrated in her fingers. She could feel time running away.

Then, leaning back, she noticed an odd bulge in the back of one of the seats. She pressed against it and felt something hard shift underneath the fabric. She retrieved the knife she had discarded earlier and began cutting into the back of the seat.

"What's she doing?" Nunez demanded, his voice growing hysterical as he started to rise. "She can't—"

Callaway shoved him back down. "Stay on the ground!"

Harley kept cutting to reveal several Ziploc bags packed with aqua-colored shards. She fished one out, smiling as she held it up for Callaway to see.

"*That* is a thing of beauty," Callaway murmured.

"I don't know how it got there," Nunez answered automatically.

"No?" Harley said, setting the bag aside. She pulled out another. "What about this one? Or this one? Do you realize how many years you can get for this?"

"It's not my vehicle," Nunez replied stonily, sticking to his script. But the energy had drained out of him. It was clear he knew where this was heading.

"There *is* one piece of good news for you in all this, though," Harley continued. "Believe it or not, we didn't come here to bust you for distribution."

Nunez stared at her, his face now a careful mask of indifference.

"Tell us about Holy Hope," she added.

He blinked a few times, as if not comprehending. "Holy Hope? What about it?"

"You used to live there, didn't you?"

He shrugged. "Yeah, so what?"

"Why'd they kick you out?" Callaway said.

Nunez shrugged again. "Hell if I know. They're racists, that's why."

Callaway clucked his tongue. "Come on, Hector. You might as well level with us. You realized how welcoming Holy Hope is of people with checkered pasts, and you saw a business opportunity."

Nunez rubbed the top of his head and winced. "You got an aspirin or something? My head's killing me."

Callaway's voice was low and dangerous. "Why don't you tell us about Sienna Davis and Eleanor Renfrew?"

Nunez blinked. "Those chicks? Barely knew them. They lived just outside the community, so they weren't really part of things."

"What about Isla Clemente?" Harley added.

A bemused grin pulled at the corner of Nunez's mouth. "Yeah, I remember her. Nice piece. A little unsettled in the head, know what I mean, but easy on the eyes."

Harley saw the muscles of Callaway's jaw bulge. Afraid things could get out of control in a hurry, she decided to manage the conversation.

"Unsettled in the head?" she said.

Nunez shrugged one shoulder. "She had this thing about distrusting men."

"Is that why she turned you down?"

"Look, all I did was offer her a job, okay? Ain't my fault if she was too stupid to know a good thing when she saw one."

"I bet that made you angry, didn't it?" Callaway pressed. "That kind of rejection? Then, next thing you know, they're kicking you out of the community. Must have really ruffled your feathers."

"Hell, yeah, it did!"

"And you decided you were going to get back at them. You started with Sienna and Eleanor because they were easier targets, living off by themselves, is that right?"

A look of confusion came over Nunez's face. "Targets? What the hell—"

"But they weren't enough, were they?" Callaway continued, gaining steam. "You got a taste for killing, didn't you? So you went back, and who better to target than the girl who rejected you to your face? Did you intend to grab Beverly, too, or did she just get in the way?"

Nunez glanced at Harley with a bewildered, pleading expression. "I don't have a clue what you're talking about! You've gotta believe me! I was angry, sure, but them kicking me out was the best thing that ever happened to me. I've done ten times more business out here than I ever could have done back there!"

The two agents exchanged a glance. Harley had a sinking feeling.

"You telling me all those women are dead?" Nunez said. "Like someone's been *hunting* them?"

"Don't play dumb," Callaway growled, but there was no conviction left in his voice.

Nunez shook his head. "I've done some bad things in my life, but I'm no murderer, okay?"

"Where were you last night?" Harley said.

"Right here, in Los Muertos. You want witnesses, collaboration? There's about five people in town who'll tell you I've been here all week."

"You expect us to take the word of some meth fiends?" Callaway said.

"They don't do meth—not all of them. Besides, they don't know what the hell's going on, so why would they lie? If I thought the law was coming down on me, you think I'd be out here coaching witnesses instead of jumping the border?"

The two agents looked at one another. No matter how much they wanted Nunez to be their man, he was looking less and less viable as a suspect. Unless his alibi proved to be a flat-out lie, or his witnesses proved to be far less reliable than Nunez thought, they had to clear him as a suspect.

The prospect stung Harley. It was the old "one step forward, two steps back" routine. If Nunez was not a killer, then they had just squandered precious time they could have used to look for the two missing girls.

They heard the siren of an approaching ambulance. Harley watched it climb the slope toward them, attended by several squad cars. She reminded herself that following leads, even when they didn't pan out, was a necessary part of the process, but it didn't make her feel any better.

Nunez was still complaining of chest pain when the ambulance arrived. Just to be safe, they loaded him on a stretcher and guided him into the back of the ambulance.

"One of these days," Harley said as the ambulance doors closed, "we're going to track down a suspect, and he's going to confess to the whole thing."

"That would be nice," Callaway replied. "But in this case, I'm not sure a confession would do us any good. Like he said, business is booming. Why would he risk that on some revenge mission?"

Harley sighed, disappointed. "At least we know where to find him if his alibi doesn't hold up."

They were both silent, watching as the ambulance pulled away. Harley's adrenaline had cooled, and she tried to stave off her disappointment by mentally going over the details of the case again, searching for a loose end, a thread she could pull on to unravel the knot even a little.

"Two former Holy Hope members have been murdered," she said, "and two current members have gone missing. I don't know if the killer is a community member or an outsider, but either way he has his eye on Holy Hope. We need to go back again, learn everything we can."

"You think there'll be another attack?"

She paused, gathering her thoughts. "I think that if there is another attack, it'll be at Holy Hope—which is why we should be there."

CHAPTER FOURTEEN

"Where is everybody?" Harley said as they entered Holy Hope for the second time in as many days. "It's as quiet as a graveyard here."

Unlike their previous visit, there was no crowd of children to greet them as they rolled along the dirt road between the houses. Nobody was out attending the gardens, either. It was as if everyone had simply disappeared.

"A communal meeting, maybe?" Callaway suggested. "With the murders and disappearances, they might want to talk things over amongst themselves."

Harley considered this, then shook her head. "I think that's what the firepit in the center is for. But nobody's there. They must be somewhere else."

It sent a chill through her. She wondered if maybe the residents had marched into town to harass Sheriff Santiago again. But if they had, wouldn't Santiago have called her?

She twisted her neck, looking back at the row of vehicles parked near the entrance to the community: four vehicles, each at least a decade old. There wasn't room to park a fifth.

Callaway pulled over and turned off the engine. "We'd better have a look around," he said, opening his door.

As Harley stepped out of the vehicle, she was struck by how much was missing from Holy Hope—not just the people, but other signs of civilization as well: telephone poles, mailboxes, electric meters, lamp posts. She tried to imagine what it would be like living so close to the land, depending so much on one's skills and the contributions of one's neighbors. She could imagine the sense of freedom: tracking time by the sun rather than a phone or a clock, checking the weather by stepping out the door instead of opening an app, not having to worry about scammers, telemarketers, prank calls, and some of the other nuisances that came with civilization.

But they still have to worry about killers, she mused. *There is no lifestyle beyond the reach of evil.*

"Where do we start?" Callaway said, planting his hands on his hips and making a slow survey of the town.

A voice answered, "How about you start by explaining why you

83

haven't found the killer yet?"

Harley turned around to see Melissa Hargrave striding toward them, her floral dress swishing around her knees. Her eyebrows were pulled together in an expression of both concern and impatience.

Gardenia stopped a few paces away and crossed her arms, looking from one agent to the other. "Or have you come to say you've solved the case?" she added.

"We're still investigating," Harley answered, taken aback by the woman's belligerence. "I promised I'd keep you aware of any new developments, and I intend to keep that promise."

Gardenia frowned as if she had missed something. "Then why are you here? Shouldn't you be out there, looking for the killer? Or are you going to tell me you think the killer's one of us?"

"We don't have any suspects at present, ma'am," Callaway said. "But all four women – both the two victims and the teenage girls who've gone missing – were connected with Holy Hope, so we need to have another look around."

Gardenia gave a cool shrug. "You won't find anything. I'm telling you, the person you're looking for isn't part of this community. He's a lone wolf who thinks he's found a herd of untended sheep, and he'll keep picking us off until he learns our teeth are just as sharp as his."

The words troubled Harley. She wondered how Gardenia could be so certain. Was it wishful thinking, the way parents often rushed to deny charges of guilt against their children?

"Ms. Hargrave," she said, "I couldn't help noticing how quiet it is today. Where is everyone?"

Gardenia gestured vaguely into the distance. "Searching the woods, the hills. That's where Isla and Bev went missing. We decided to take matters into our own hands, since you seem to be too busy."

Harley had to stifle a groan. She thought of Gardenia's threat back at the sheriff's office about arming everyone in the community. It would certainly fall within the category of taking matters into their own hands.

While Harley was still contemplating a delicate way to respond, she noticed the sandals Gardenia was wearing. She couldn't help noticing how different they looked from Eleanor's sneakers.

"Mind if I ask where you got your shoes?" she said.

Gardenia squinted, looking puzzled. "My shoes? We have someone who makes them right here in Holy Hope—his father was a tailor."

"Do a lot of people here wear them?"

"Everyone does. Shoes wear out. Why spend your hard-earned

84

money at Wal-Mart when you can get a handmade pair in exchange for a few chores?"

Harley glanced at Callaway, wondering if he understood the significance. Recognition came into his eyes, and he nodded. Eleanor's shoes had not only been too big for her, but probably had never belonged to her in the first place.

Which means...what? Harley thought. *The killer has a thing about swapping shoes with his victims? He didn't do it with Sienna.*

Not sure what to make of this information, she decided to file it away for later.

"I'm sorry, Ms. Hargrave," Callaway interrupted, "but what did you say everyone is doing?"

"They're searching for evidence, for clues. Maybe those two girls were chased off into the woods and we can find their trail. We have quite a few talented trackers among our group."

Harley was about to ask if Gardenia had any thoughts on where Isla and Beverly might have gone when a scream ripped across the hillside, sending chills down Harley's back. She looked at Callaway. Then, jolted into action, the two agents sprinted toward the sound.

"He's back!" she heard Gardenia cry behind her. "He's killed again!"

CHAPTER FIFTEEN

Harley's legs burned, and she could hear Callaway huffing beside her like an angry bull. Sweat beaded on her forehead and ran down her ribcage like bullets.

She glanced over her shoulder and was surprised to see Gardenia lagging only a short distance behind them, a testament to how well her lifestyle kept her in shape. The hem of her dress was bunched to the side in one hand, revealing her muscular calves. Her face was locked in determination.

They found a knot of people gathered at the edge of a potato field, one of the numerous crop fields hidden behind the houses. Dark green leaves sprouted in perfectly-straight rows, each separated from the next by a trench so that the field rippled like waves on a lake. In the corner of this field, a number of immature potato plants lay overturned around a large mound of earth, breaking the perfect pattern.

Harley and Callaway came up short as they caught sight of the mound, which had been disturbed just enough to reveal a pair of bodies, one face-up and the other facedown. At a glance, Harley could see they were young, female, and recently deceased.

Harley's heart sank. It was as if a nightmare had suddenly sprung to life. The very thing she had feared – that the two missing women would wind up dead before Harley could find them – had come true. It was enough to make her feel sick.

A crowd of onlookers, perhaps twenty in all, stood around the bodies in a semicircle, shocked into silence. A tall, middle-aged man with a white beard shook his head.

"No," he murmured, his voice hollow, his eyes looking puzzled at the sight. "No, no, no." Then he turned abruptly and, as the crowd separated, he hurried back toward the buildings.

Harley considered raising her voice to tell him to come back—they would need to interview everyone, after all. Then again, they knew where to find him, didn't they? It wasn't likely he would be going far.

Callaway set his hand on Harley's shoulder. "I'll call it in," he said gently.

She nodded gratefully as a sense of queasiness roiled in her gut. It wasn't the sight of the bodies that upset her—she had seen plenty in her time with the Bureau, and she wouldn't have been able to do her job if she had been squeamish about death. It was the sense of personal responsibility that sickened her.

I could have prevented this, she thought. *If I had done things a little differently, paid more attention to the details...*

Gardenia brushed past her and fell to her knees in the dirt, shaking one of the bodies as if to wake it. "Isla! Can you hear me, Isla? You need to tell us who did this to you!"

Harley took Gardenia by the arm. "Ma'am, this is an active crime scene. I need you to—"

Gardenia rose and spun toward Harley, her eyes dark and accusing. "You see?" she exclaimed, glancing toward the crowd to make sure everyone was paying attention. "This is what your hard work and good intentions get us. This is on *you*, Agent Cole! *You're* responsible!"

Harley faltered, not sure what to say. "None of us wanted this outcome," she managed.

Gardenia looked around at the gathered crowd, sneering. "None of us could prevent it, either—no one except you. Because that's your job, isn't it? If you can't stop this from happening, what the hell are you doing here?"

Harley stared back into the older woman's face, her cheeks burning with shame. She felt the words sink down inside her like poisonous rain.

Then Callaway stepped in front of Gardenia. "Ma'am," he said, "I'm going to have to ask you to step aside. This isn't the time for pointing fingers. Right now the only person deserving blame is the killer, and I can assure you that person is not Harley Cole."

"Their blood is on your hands," Gardenia hissed, driving the nail home. Then she moved away, her head erect as she pushed through the crowd of onlookers.

Callaway turned his attention to Harley, who was staring blankly at the bodies. He snapped his fingers in front of her face.

"Hey," he said. "Stay in the game. We might be down, but time hasn't run out yet."

Her voice was faint, as if coming from a long distance away. "It's not a game, Callaway. These two girls were taken on my watch. I should have posted a patrol here, should have kept eyes on the community."

Callaway shook his head. "The first two victims lived outside the community. We had no reason to think the killer was targeting these people. We didn't even know whether he would kill again."

"But he did, Callaway," Harley said bleakly. "And that's on me."

Callaway took her by the shoulders and stared into her eyes. "It's on *us*, Harley. We're both working this case, and that means we share both the credit and the blame. I wish we'd prevented this, too, but blaming yourself will only compromise your ability to stop the *next* murder. So instead of beating yourself up for something we can't change, I need you to focus on catching this guy so we don't have to find any more bodies."

Harley knew he was right. She needed to pull herself together. As much as she would have preferred to have found these two girls alive, the cold reality was that the killer had just given the investigation a much-needed jolt. There was no telling how much evidence he might have left behind.

She felt a surge of gratitude toward Callaway. Had they been alone, she would have liked to put her arms around him. But he was right: This wasn't the time for blame. There was too much work to be done.

"Can you do that?" he said, studying her closely. "Because if you need a few minutes…" He trailed off. What was he going to suggest, that she go back to the car and have a good cry?

She shook her head, pulling herself together with an effort. "I'm good. I'll have my pity party later."

Callaway's gaze lingered on her a few moments longer. Then he nodded, satisfied. "Okay," he said. "I'm relieved to hear that, because we've got our work cut out for us."

That's an understatement, if I ever heard one, Harley thought.

Turning her full attention to the situation at hand, Harley studied the soft earth along the field, which looked like it had been trampled by a herd of buffalo. The crowd of spectators stood only a few paces from the bodies, which meant they could be destroying evidence every time they shifted their feet.

"I need everyone to move back!" she said in a loud voice, raising her hands. "I know you're in shock, but we have to preserve the crime scene!"

The crowd retreated, murmuring to one another, and Harley advanced, driving them back about fifty feet. They watched her warily, keeping their voices low, still sounding more shocked than angry. That was good. Harley couldn't afford them getting out of hand, not when she and Callaway were the only two on the scene.

"No closer," she warned them. "If you want us to catch the killer, keep your distance. There's no telling how much evidence he may have left."

Or how much these people may already have destroyed, she thought dismally as her gaze panned across the disturbed earth. Then, recalling her earlier conversation with Gardenia, she studied the footwear of the community members. Sandals, all of them—which meant that if they eliminated the community members' tracks, as well as any she and Callaway may have left, the remaining prints would probably belong to the killer.

She just hoped they hadn't been entirely obscured.

Deciding she had made her point, Harley returned to Callaway.

"How soon will forensics be here?" she said.

"Half-hour, give or take," Callaway answered. He was taking pictures of the scene on his phone. There was no telling how much the scene had already been contaminated, but at least the pictures would provide a frame of reference in case anything was disturbed further.

"Probably shouldn't walk around, at least not in the field," Harley said. The earth bordering the field was dry clay, unlikely to remember much. Still, there was no telling when a faint, partial footprint might prove crucial to an investigation.

Callaway finished taking pictures and slipped the phone into his back pocket. "He's not screwing around. Four bodies in as many days?"

"Most serials have cycles of activity and inactivity," Harley observed. "They scratch the itch, then disappear for a while until they can't help but do it again. We might see the same pattern here."

"We might," Callaway agreed. "Or he might be just getting started."

The question is, Harley thought, *who's he going to grab next?*

CHAPTER SIXTEEN

The forensic team, clad in HAZMAT suits, carefully brushed the dirt from the bodies, pausing now and again to take pictures with the camera mounted on a tripod nearby. Harley watched, arms folded, reminding herself to be patient.

The problem was, she had already been waiting for hours. The forensics van had gotten bogged down in a sinkhole, and they'd been forced to wait for a tow truck to pull them out. The afternoon was getting late, and Harley couldn't help feeling discouraged that they were no closer to catching the killer than before.

"Anything interesting?" Callaway said, coming up behind her. He regarded the scene with a thoughtful expression.

"Hard to see much," Harley answered. "I should have gotten better seats."

The joke was in poor taste, and Harley regretted it as soon as she'd said it. Some agents made a habit of such jokes as a way of distancing themselves from the humanity of the situation—and thus from any unpleasant feelings. They were the same agents who preferred talking about "perps" and "vics" to using real names. That had never been Harley's way, however. It was the very humanity of the killings that drove her to find the killer.

Callaway nodded, acknowledging the joke, but he seemed to find as little humor in it as Harley did.

Harley, wishing to move on, said, "Anyone see anything?" She nodded toward the crowd of spectators a stone's throw away. While waiting for the forensics team to arrive, Callaway had conducted interviews, pencil and paper in hand, getting down as many details as possible before the memories were corrupted by time. From his frustrated expression, however, Harley guessed he hadn't learned much that was useful.

"Tight-lipped, all of them," he answered. "Can't help but wonder what Ms. Hargrave told them. They seem to think we're just as likely to help the killer as to stop him."

"Well, these two were killed on our watch. We couldn't have saved the first pair, but Isla and Bev..." she trailed off.

"You're doing it again. That thing where you blame yourself for not being Superwoman."

"I'm not blaming myself. I'm just explaining why they don't trust us. If they knew how often investigators have no leads to go on and nothing to do but wait for the killer to strike again, hoping he'll make a mistake…" she trailed off, hoping they would not find themselves in the same situation. She had joined the Bureau to stop murderers, not to do damage control after the fact.

Callaway rested his hand on her shoulder. "We'll get him, Harley. Sooner or later, his number will come up."

She nodded, grateful for his attempt to encourage her, though she did not feel any better. Then she spotted a teenage girl lingering at the front of the crowd. It was the same girl she had seen during their first visit to Holy Hope, the one with the basket of vegetables who had hurried away from the agents when they tried to question her.

A look of fear came into the girl's eyes as her gaze met Harley's. She ducked her head and turned around, pushing through the crowd.

"Hold that thought," Harley murmured, moving away from Callaway.

As Harley neared the spectators, she saw the young girl slip through the back of the crowd, casting a worried glance over her shoulder as she hurried down toward the buildings. She moved at a quick clip, just short of a run.

"Wait a minute!" Harley called. "I just want to talk!"

The girl stopped dead in her tracks. She stood there immobile, her back to Harley, holding her right elbow with her left hand in a classic pose of insecurity. She looked frozen, as if Harley's words had some overpowering hold on her.

"Why were you trying to get away?" Harley said as she caught up.

The girl's thick, dark hair hung across her face in a curtain, hiding her features. She said nothing, like a guilty child caught stealing candy.

Harley knew she had to find a way to disarm this girl's defenses. She spoke in a tone that was direct but also gentle, and low enough that nobody nearby would overhear.

"What's your name?"

"Violet." She cleared her throat, then said it a little more loudly. "Violet."

"Were you there when the bodies were found, Violet?"

The girl was silent for several heartbeats. Then her words spilled out in a torrent. "I didn't know what it was—I thought an animal had gotten into the potatoes or something. I didn't mean to disturb anything, honestly!"

That was when Harley noticed the dirt crusted beneath Violet's fingernails. She remembered the scream that had drawn her and Callaway to the field.

Poor girl, she thought. *To come across the bodies that way. And she's about the same age, too.*

"You're not at fault for anything," she assured Violet. "You did the right thing, calling for help. Without you, there's no telling how long it would have been before someone found them."

She waited. The girl remained as she was, rigid, her chest moving in quick, shallow breaths.

"How well did you know Isla and Bev?" Harley said.

Violet's eyes cut toward the crowd—searching for Gardenia, Harley supposed. Harley leaned to the side, blocking the girl's view. She knew firsthand how threatening Gardenia's gaze could be, and she didn't need Violet any more intimidated than she already was.

"Pretty well, I guess," Violet answered. "We were friends, sort of."

"Sort of?"

She shrugged. "You kind of have to be friends when you live this close to everyone, don't you?"

"So you weren't close?"

The girl's long, lank hair shivered as she shook her head. "I keep to myself a lot." She hung her head as if this were a shameful admission. Then she added, "I talked to Bev now and then, but not really Isla."

"What did you and Bev talk about?"

Violet shrugged. "Nothing much. Our old lives, occasionally. Gardenia doesn't really like us to talk about what happened before we got here...but sometimes you have to, you know?"

Harley nodded sympathetically. "Your past doesn't go away just because your circumstances change."

The girl crossed her arms and stared at the ground, as if waiting for the next question.

"Was Bev dating anyone?" Harley said.

Violet looked up, frowning. "Dating? No, we're not allowed to date, not until we're eighteen. That's one of the rules here."

This struck Harley as a bit old-fashioned. "And you go along with that? You know they can't *make* you follow that rule."

The girl lowered her voice as if confiding a secret. "Yeah, but they can throw you out. Where would I go? What would I do? These people are the only family I have, and trust me, there are a lot more rules when you live in one of those foster homes."

"You're a smart girl. You could make it on your own, if you wanted

92

to."

Violet gave her a half-hearted smile, as if to say she was grateful for the compliment but didn't really believe it.

"Anyway," Violet continued, "Bev had a few crushes, but she was careful. She didn't really go on anything you could call a date, and she never would have gotten involved with the wrong guy."

Harley would have liked to continue this line of questioning, but she knew that any moment Gardenia might march over and end the conversation. Harley needed to cover as much ground as she could as quickly as she could.

"What about Isla?" she said. "I heard a rumor she was a bit standoffish around men. Is that true?"

Violet gave her a worried look. "Yeah, I guess. She didn't like most men."

"Really?" Harley pressed. "Attractive girl like her? There wasn't anyone in town she was going with?"

The girl bit her lip. "I probably shouldn't talk about it. It's just a rumor."

Harley wasn't going to let her off that easily. "What rumor?" she said.

Violet hesitated. Harley sensed a silent war going on behind the girl's eyes. Should she trust the federal agent with the truth, or might it come back to haunt her?

Finally Violet swallowed hard and said, "Bev was worried about Isla because she thought Isla was seeing someone. It was weird, because Isla was so shy around guys—not to mention how much trouble she'd be in if anyone found out she was breaking the rules."

"Did Bev say who this mysterious stranger was?"

Violet shook her head.

"Was it someone in the community?" Harley pressed. She could see Violet was near her breaking point, but she needed more to go on than a vague suggestion that one of the victims might have been dating someone.

Violet closed her eyes, a pained expression on her face. "All she said was that she didn't like him because he was too old for Isla."

Before Harley could respond, the girl's eyes opened and cut toward the crowd again. "I really need to get going," she said, pulling away from Harley. "I'm sorry I can't help more."

Harley opened her mouth to protest, but the girl was already gone, trotting away like a child half her age.

A young woman in a little girl's body, Harley thought. Holy Hope was a community of refugees—survivors of abuse, addiction, bullying. It reminded Harley of that line about the Statue of Liberty: "Give me your tired, your poor, your huddled masses yearning to breathe free, the wretched refuse of your teeming shore." It was a humanitarian organization in that sense, a beacon of hope in a dark world.

And yet…why couldn't Harley shake the feeling something was wrong there, something false? Why did she sense that behind the mask of happiness and simplicity was a darker guise, a guise Melissa Hargrave didn't want her to see?

A hand touched her shoulder, startling her.

"Someone's jumpy," Callaway said. "Learn anything from your new friend?"

Harley frowned, troubled. "It sounds like Isla may have been seeing an older man."

"Somewhere here in the community?"

"I'm not sure. I'd ask Ms. Hargrave, but I'm pretty sure any goodwill we might have built with her disappeared when she saw what was in that potato field."

"You think she's hiding something." It was a statement rather than a question.

Harley hesitated. "I think she's hiding a lot of things. I just don't know if any of them have anything to do with our investigation, and we're not going to learn anything by badgering her."

They both fell silent. Harley's mind drifted back to Violet's words. Was it possible Isla had been involved with an older man, perhaps a predator who had infiltrated the community under a false name? Maybe things with Isla got too physical, and when Bev interfered, the killer murdered both of them. This much was conceivable. But what about the first two murders?

Prompted by a fresh idea, Harley returned to the potato field, where the forensic team had just finished uncovering the two bodies. They lay side by side on their backs, the dirt carefully brushed away to reveal a pair of faces that looked almost angelic in their youth and paleness. Isla Clemente's body was nearly unharmed, except for the pattern of bruises on her throat, but the side of Beverly Morris's head was a bloody mess of clumped hair, skull fragments, and exposed brain matter.

"Isla was strangled, just like Sienna," Callaway observed, his voice hard. There was an undercurrent of anger just beneath the words.

"But not Bev," Harley answered, sickened by the sight of Beverly's mangled skull. "He beat her senseless."

"And then kept going a while longer."

Harley's eyes traveled down the length of the two bodies. "No signs of sexual assault," she murmured. "If sex had been the primary motivation for the murders, you'd expect some degree of violation."

"It wouldn't make sense to target pairs, either," Callaway agreed. "It happens once, that might be a coincidence. But twice in a row?"

The same thing had already occurred to Harley. Sexual predators were experts at isolating their victims. It was much easier to maintain control when there was only one person to dominate.

As Harley contemplated the possibilities, her eyes continued down to the teenagers' feet. Both teenagers were wearing sandals, just like those of the other community members. There was something strange, however, about one of Isla's feet.

"Look at the angle of Isla's right foot," Harley said.

Callaway squatted down so he could examine it more closely. "Ankle's broken. Probably happened while she was running."

And it was probably the reason the killer caught her, Harley thought. She imagined Isla running through the trees, scared for her life, screaming for help. She would have done plenty of screaming when she broke her ankle, that was for sure. The question was, why hadn't anybody heard her?

Harley took a deep breath and let it out, rubbing wearily at her face. "Let's go over it again," she said. "What do the victims have in common so far?"

Callaway thought. "They're all female. All connected with Holy Hope."

"But different ages, different backgrounds, different appearances— different hair color, hairstyles, height, weight, everything. What commonalities are there other than gender?"

"There's the fact that he's killing in pairs."

Harley paused, considering this. "How did he take them both without anyone hearing so much as a scream? You've seen how close all the houses are together, and it's not as if they're airtight."

"Maybe they were already in the woods when he found them," Callaway suggested.

"What would they be doing out there at night? Taking a stroll?"

Callaway shrugged. "Maybe."

"How does our killer get his hands on both of them? One of them is bound to run."

Callaway was silent for a few beats. Then his eyebrows rose as a new thought occurred to him.

"Didn't Gardenia say Bev had a limp?" he said. "Maybe the killer gets his hands on Isla, then chases Bev down before she can get back to the community."

Harley considered. After a few moments, however, she shook her head, not buying Callaway's theory. "It takes a long time to strangle a person the way he strangled Isla. Even if Beverly's limp was bad enough to slow her to a crawl, she could have hidden. She would have been doing everything in her power to escape. There's no way she would have made it that easy for him."

Callaway shoved his hands into his pockets as he stared down at the bodies. "What's your theory, then?" he said.

Harley's gaze went from the potato field to the overlooking hills, then to the crowd of spectators nearby. Some of them had petered back to the community, but several dozen remained, conversing in low voices. Harley studied their faces one by one, wondering if she might be staring right into the eyes of the man they were hunting.

"We should be running background checks on everyone in the community," she murmured.

Callaway grunted. "Good luck getting their real identities. You might as well read a botany textbook."

It galled Harley, knowing Callaway was right. If only Gardenia and the others would cooperate, they could rule out any obvious suspects from within the community. The more Gardenia insisted the killer wasn't a member of Holy Hope, the more reason Harley had to suspect he was.

Her mind kept returning to the fact that the killer was targeting pairs of women. It was an unusual choice, not least of all because it was much riskier than isolating an individual target, and so Harley thought there was a decent chance that if the murderer had killed anyone before Sienna and Eleanor, she would be able to cross-match the crimes—and potentially shed new light on the case.

"I have an idea," she said to Callaway. "I'm going to head to the sheriff's office and do some research, dig into old news articles and see if I can't find any women who've gone missing in pairs. It's a longshot, but it's worth trying."

Callaway nodded thoughtfully. "Not a bad idea. I'm going to stick around, stay at the scene of the crime a little longer. Someone needs to keep an eye on the community."

"You think the killer will attack again?" It would be unusual for him to strike again so soon. Then again, he had already killed four women in two days, and he might be just getting started.

There was a determined gleam in Callaway's eyes. "I don't know, but if he does, I'll be waiting for him."

Harley felt a stab of guilt. Callaway was knowingly putting himself in danger, and Harley felt a sense of obligation as his partner to take the risks right alongside him. But there was no telling whether the killer would return, and she did not want to waste time waiting around, not when there was work to be done.

"Just be careful," she said, meeting his eyes. "We don't know what we're up against here."

Callaway patted his holster and smiled grimly. "Neither does he, Harley. Neither does he."

CHAPTER SEVENTEEN

Harley approached the sergeant's desk and drummed her fingers on the wood as she glanced around for someone to help her. The sheriff's office was oddly quiet: no clacking of computer keys, no ringing of phones, no murmur of idle conversation. She would have expected such a scene at lunchtime, not in the middle of the afternoon.

She was helping herself to a bowl of complimentary pretzels when a toilet flushed nearby. *Finally,* she thought, grateful someone was still around.

The man who stepped out of the restroom was young and tall, with a baby face and a pompadour hairstyle that gleamed greasily beneath the fluorescent lights. He wore a robotic expression up until the moment he noticed Harley. Then his face lit up with an eager intensity, not unlike that of a beagle whose master has just come home.

"Can I help you, ma'am?" he said, hooking his thumbs in his belt. He wore the dun-colored uniform of a sheriff's deputy. Probably new, since Harley didn't recognize him.

Harley held up her badge, happy to be able to do so now that she had it again. She had served only as a consultant on the Navarro case, and she had learned the hard way about the limitations of that role.

The deputy leaned forward, scrutinizing the badge closely. "Wow," he said, shaking his head with wonder. "A real Fed, in the flesh. Never thought I'd see the day."

Harley smiled politely. "Just a public servant, like you. Is Sheriff Santiago around?"

The deputy was still staring at the badge. He looked like he wanted to hold it, though Harley wasn't sure she'd ever get it back if she offered.

"He's downtown," the deputy answered, "carrying out an eviction notice. Something I can do for you?"

Harley tried not to let her disappointment show. She had hoped to have a few moments to talk with Santiago face-to-face about Kelly's investigation. Considering where things stood with her own investigation, she could use the boost. It appeared she would have to wait, however.

"I just need to look through your missing persons reports," she answered.

The deputy finally looked up from the badge, cocking his head curiously at her. "You working the case at that off-grid community?"

"Holy Hope, yes."

He shook his head, as if it were a lost cause. "Mighty brave of you, getting involved with them."

"Why's that?"

"They don't give two farts about the police. You won't get any help from them."

As if I didn't know that already, Harley thought. She took a more tactful approach. "That's why I'm here, hoping to find any connections with the killings."

As soon as she had spoken, she realized it had been a mistake. The deputy's eyes brightened with excitement.

"You think he's killed before?" he said.

Harley tried to downplay it, as if it were only a remote possibility. "It's a longshot. More than likely I'll come up empty-handed, but I won't know until I look. I'd really appreciate it if you could help me out."

The deputy nodded, looking disappointed she hadn't confided more. "You can use my computer. Come on, I'll show you."

Harley followed the deputy down the hall to a small cubicle cluttered with textbooks.

"I'm studying to join the SWAT team," the deputy told her, slapping the top of a book titled *Breach & Clear: A Tactician's Guide to Close-Quarters Combat.* "They're some of the baddest asses around—present company excepted, of course."

Harley smiled tightly as she pulled out the chair and sat down. As she reached for the mouse, however, the deputy grabbed it first, leaning over her shoulder so he could operate the keyboard.

"Have to log you in," he explained, his breath close to her ear. "Name's Sonny, by the way. With an *O*, not a *U*."

There was an unpleasant intimacy to his closeness. It took all Harley's concentration not to push off from the desk, shoving 'Sonny with an O' back into the cubicle behind him.

She did her best to stay friendly. "I'm Agent Cole—with a *C*, not a *K*."

His face remained blank for a moment as he typed in his credentials. Then he smiled brightly. "Ha! Good one!"

Once they were logged into the system, Sonny relinquished his hold on the mouse and stepped away. "There you go," he said, planting his hands on his hips. "That should help. Just watch out for the F key—it likes to stick."

"I'll be careful," Harley assured him.

She pulled her chair forward, making herself comfortable. Sonny remained where he was, watching.

"This could take a while," she warned, hoping he would take the hint.

The deputy, however, only shrugged his shoulders. "I've got time."

Harley was brainstorming ways she might get rid of him when his cell phone went off. He raised it to his ear, keeping his eyes on Harley.

"Yeah, what is it?"

Harley opened the database and began searching. As promised, the F key got stuck and she had to carefully pop it back up.

"Yes, I talked with him," the deputy was saying into the phone. "He insisted that was the right number for the plate, but..." He paused, listening. "Okay, I'll go over and check again."

The deputy let out a heavy sigh as he hung up the phone. "Well, party's over. Boss needs me back in the field."

He paused. Harley had the impression he was waiting for her to ask what it was.

"What kind of case?" she said, humoring him in the hope it would speed his departure.

He stretched his arms out and rolled his neck, giving a satisfied sigh as it popped. "Oh, the usual. B and E. Just another day on the job."

"Sounds serious. Sheriff Santiago must really trust you if he's putting a case like that in your hands."

He shrugged, looking secretly pleased at the implication. "It's really not a big deal. You should have been here last month—there was this case about a killer who was hiding his victims in mine shafts. Get this. I even went to the place where he lived. It was practically a palace!"

Harley feigned surprise. She made a mental note to ask Santiago about his hiring policies the next time she spoke with him. Whatever they were, they needed to be refined.

"Well," the deputy said with a regretful sigh, "I guess I'll leave you to it. Make sure to log out when you're all done."

"I'll do that."

She watched him go. When he had disappeared around the corner, she let out an audible sigh of relief. Finally, some peace and quiet.

She started by perusing old police reports, searching for anything tagged in the MISSING PERSONS category. She scrolled through two pages before deciding it would take all night to examine the entire list.

There had to be a better way.

She tried narrowing the search to reports on pairs of missing persons, but none of the keywords she tried seemed to help. She sat back, stumped.

What's the killer's signature? she mused. No two killers behaved in exactly the same way. Each one had his or her quirks, little discrepancies that set them apart—discrepancies that could sometimes be used to link crimes that did not otherwise seem to have much in common.

Harley sat up as a fresh idea came to her. On a hunch, she added the word "SHOES" to the search and pressed ENTER.

There, at the top of a short list, was a report detailing the disappearance of two sisters six months earlier, Beatrice and Bella Rasco. Police had put out a statewide APB and interviewed everyone who'd had any contact with the reclusive family, but they had failed to generate so much as a single scrap of evidence. The sisters had simply vanished. No bodies had ever been found.

There was, however, one piece of evidence of particular interest to Harley: two pairs of muddy shoes left behind in the house. This information had been logged as a tiny footnote, as if the officer on the scene had only recorded it out of a sense of obligation to be thorough.

Was it possible these two sisters had been the killer's first victims?

She sat back, tapping her fingertips on the edge of the desk. The muddy shoes were an odd detail. Maybe the sisters had each kept an extra pair of work shoes for getting dirty. They might have swapped them out and left voluntarily—crossed the border into Mexico, perhaps, to start a new life. Leaving shoes behind was not exactly a reliable marker of foul play.

No, but it's an odd coincidence.

Intrigued now, Harley entered the address of the sisters' farmhouse into Google Maps. To her surprise, it was located on Sawyer Pass, just down the road from the house in which Sienna Davis and Eleanor Renfrew had lived.

Now that has to be more than a coincidence, she thought, growing more excited the longer she thought about it.

The difference here, of course, was that the bodies of the sisters had never been found—no small feat, considering they had gone missing half a year earlier. If they were indeed dead, which was still just an assumption at this point, could they really have been the victims of the same man who had so clumsily disposed of the bodies of Isla Clemente and Beverly Morris in a shallow grave at the edge of a potato field?

And what about Sienna Davis and Eleanor Renfrew? The killer had left their bodies at the side of the road, as if it made no difference to him whether they were found or when.

It was backwards. Killers' methods tended to evolve as they became more proficient in their work; but in this case the killer – if he had started with the Rasco sisters – had gotten more sloppy over time. More desperate, perhaps.

Was it possible there was more than one killer at work? It would explain the change in MOs.

You're wandering too far afield, she told herself. *Don't get lost in the weeds.*

Leaning forward again, she searched the area around the Rascos' home for any sources of water. As she had expected, she found nothing—the closest creek was some fifty miles away, well beyond walking distance.

It was a high, dry area. So where had the mud come from?

She heard a door open, followed by a bray of laughter. Sonny was back. Time to get going.

Harley logged out of the database and rose, hurrying down the hall. As she turned the corner, she heard Sonny say something behind her, but she continued on as if she hadn't heard him.

She needed to see that farmhouse for herself. It just might be where their killer had learned his trade.

CHAPTER EIGHTEEN

Skink rocked back and forth, his arms wrapped around his legs as he watched all the bright lights of the vehicles from a nearby hill.

How amusing it was, seeing them puzzling over the mystery he had left them! How serious their faces looked! He could not see them well now, but earlier he had crept close, before all the bright lights had arrived. There had only been two officers, a man and a woman. They weren't police officers, but they carried guns and badges, so they were probably working for the government.

FBI? CIA? ATF? Skink did not know, and he did not much care. What mattered was that he had done what he set out to do, and the voices were quiet again.

For now.

He held up his hand, studying the dirt buried beneath the nails. He was listening for the faintest echo of those voices deep down in the well of his mind, a sure sign that their spirits had taken on new bodies. For the moment, he heard nothing.

Still...he *sensed* them there, waiting for the right opportunity to come back and haunt him again. They would not stop. He had to stay ahead of them, strike before they had a chance to occupy new bodies—that way they would be stranded and have no choice but to move on to whatever place the dead were supposed to go. And then...then...

Then they'll leave me alone, forever. Then it will finally be quiet.

He could not imagine this possibility (he had lived with their voices all his life, after all, so he had never before experienced a reality in which they didn't haunt him), but he had to believe it was possible. They'd had the upper hand in life, but he would not let them have the upper hand in death.

A soft breeze caressed his face, wicking away the sweat. He closed his eyes. No sooner had he done so than he saw their faces—not just their first faces, but the ones that came later as well. Every time he killed, he thought he was done with them, but the voices always came back.

"That's because you were clumsy," he muttered to himself, unaware he was speaking aloud. "It has to be both together, at once, for it to really work, but that's too much to ask, isn't it?"

The critical tone of his own voice reminded him of theirs, and he felt a sudden chill, the kind Momma had once told him meant a goose had stepped on his grave.

Three times he had goofed it up, but there would not be a fourth. No, this time he would be more careful, make sure they were both good and ready before he banished them from the world for good. Only then would he have peace.

Skink stood and stretched lazily, like a cat in the sunlight. If anyone had looked up at that moment, they would have seen him standing there on the hillside, watching. But nobody did. They were as busy as ants after a storm. If only they knew the storm wasn't over.

"If at first you don't succeed," he murmured, "try, try again."

CHAPTER NINETEEN

Harley leaned on the steering wheel as she stared at the dilapidated farmhouse, a pool of shadow in the deepening night. She checked her phone again, but it only confirmed what she already knew: This was the house in which Beatrice and Bella Rasco had lived all their adult lives until they went missing.

Studying the rundown building, it was difficult to imagine anyone ever having lived there. The door hung drunkenly, one hinge ready to tear free, and several of the windows were covered with long pine planks, grayed and warped by sunlight. Weeds grew riotously along the foundation.

It's like a scene from Hansel and Gretel, Harley mused. *I bet the witch is in there fattening up Hansel right this moment.*

She had simply assumed the house would have new owners by now, but it didn't look as if anyone had lived there since the sisters went missing. She was surprised the county hadn't demolished the building in the interest of public safety. Maybe they had forgotten it existed.

As she began to get out of the car, it occurred to her that she should probably call Callaway. He would want to know where she was, after all. Besides, this could be dangerous—there was no telling where the floor might give way beneath her if she went inside, or even whether the whole building would collapse like a house of cards when she tugged on the door.

She navigated to her contacts and pressed on Callaway's name. Then she paused, her finger hovering over the CALL button. She played out the conversation in her head. She would tell him where she was and describe the house, and what would he say in response?

He'd tell me to wait till he gets here, because that's how to do things by the book.

Or, just as bad, he might send a patrol car. It was one thing to waste her own time on a wild goose chase, but quite another to waste someone else's time. She didn't care to be the butt of any jokes.

Besides, it didn't look as if anyone had been at the farmhouse in years. What did she have to worry about? Callaway was the one waiting for the killer to show up. He was in far greater danger than she was.

There's nothing in that house I can't handle.

She slipped her phone back into her pocket and approached the house. As she neared the front door, something rustled in the grass near her feet. She turned on the mini flashlight she kept on her keychain and scanned the yard, but she saw nothing except a yellowing sock half-swallowed by dirt, and a headless, naked doll spotted with burn marks that might have come from cigarettes.

Harley felt a shiver of revulsion.

Despite her confidence in the house's abandonment, she knocked anyway. The door shuddered, its upper hinge creaking with rust. A cool breeze caressed the nape of Harley's neck, like the breath of a ghost leaning over her shoulder.

"Anyone home? I'm with the FBI!"

Feeling silly waiting for an answer, Harley pressed the latch and tried to open the door. To her surprise, however, she found it locked—or blocked. She could not tell which. Either way, the door did not budge even when she pressed her hip against it. It struck her as strange, since people this far off the beaten path rarely locked their doors, at least in her experience.

Unless it's been shut up since the sisters disappeared, she mused, taking a step back. She stared up at the remains of the chimney, a few courses of crumbling brick with a gap like a missing tooth. There was no smoke, not that she had expected to see any.

Harley moved toward the back of the house, hopeful she might find another entrance. Along the way, she tried peering through the windows that had not been boarded over, but the glass was covered in a build-up of grease, grime, and soot so thick as to make them opaque. They didn't look like they'd been washed since Lincoln's presidency.

The wind stirred, and the leaves of the nearby aspens made a dry, reedy sound as they rasped together. One of the wooden shingles lifted, exposing a black mouth, and closed again. Bats flitted about the eaves, snatching their unsuspecting prey with terrible speed.

As Harley reached the rear of the house, she noticed an SUV parked in the woods. She approached it, the beam of her flashlight turning milky as it touched the windshield, which was covered in a thick film of dust and pollen. The tires had sunk several inches into the ground, the rubber cracked and brittle. The vehicle clearly had not moved in quite some time.

She was about to return to the house when she heard a grunt nearby. Panning her flashlight across the open ground behind the house, she spotted a wooden fence running far back into the woods. Curious now, she moved closer and leaned on one of the rickety boards, peering toward the back of the enclosure.

There was a low shelter built of wooden pallets among the trees. She thought she sensed movement inside it, but she could not be sure. Then, on instinct, she turned the flashlight off and waited.

Nothing happened.

Just as she was beginning to feel as if this whole visit had been a waste of time, she noticed a triangular dinner bell hanging from one of the fence boards. She picked up the striker, which hung from a nail, and tentatively batted it against the sides of the triangle.

While the first note was still ringing in the air, there was a sudden rush of movement from the shelter as a swarm of pigs rushed out, squealing and jostling one another. They pressed up against the fence, shoving their snouts through the gaps, nostrils flapping like feeble wings.

Harley staggered back, startled, and clicked on her flashlight again. The animals looked more like dogs than pigs, they were so skinny. Their sides were shrunken, causing their hips and the coarse hair on their backs to stand out. Their heads looked swollen by contrast.

Maybe this place isn't quite so abandoned as I thought.

The pigs looked sickly, sure, but someone had to be feeding them *something* for them to still be alive. Had the sisters left the pigs to a neighbor down the road, or maybe a family friend?

Harley reached carefully toward one of the larger pigs. It grunted, bucking her hand with its snout. Then, as her hand dropped again, it made a tentative effort to bite her finger. She pulled back with a gasp.

They're just hungry, she told herself. *You'd eat just about anything if you were starving, too.*

Still, she felt grateful to have the fence between her and them.

Suddenly her phone rang, causing her to jerk as if shocked by an electric current. The pigs watched her expectantly with their beady eyes as she answered.

"Where are you?" Callaway said without any greeting. He sounded troubled, and Harley immediately felt on edge.

"Not far from you," she answered, moving away as one of the pigs began to squeal. "What's going on?"

She expected Callaway to remark on the background noise. If he had heard it, however, he did not seem to care.

"I need you back at Holy Hope as soon as you can make it."

Harley felt a stirring of dread. "Why? What's going on?"

His words confirmed the very thing she had feared.

"Bad news," he answered solemnly. "Another woman has been taken."

CHAPTER TWENTY

Harley found Callaway standing beside his truck just past the sign reading "HOLY HOPE COMMUNITY: ALL ARE WELCOME." The cheerful colors looked garish in the glow of the headlights, and Harley couldn't help wondering just how welcoming these people felt knowing there was a killer picking them off two by two.

Harley rolled down her window as she pulled up beside Callaway. "Should I park here?" she said.

Callaway nodded, his face grave. "Everyone's just up the hill. We can walk."

Harley shifted into park and turned off the engine, mentally preparing herself for what was next. In most investigations, there were long lulls between those moments the tabloids might dub as the "highlights" of the case: the discovery of a body or a murder weapon, the disappearance of a possible victim, the identification of a potential suspect. Though the work was never done, these lulls gave investigators a chance to recover from the emotional intensity of examining the bodies of victims, interviewing grieving family members, and interrogating suspects. In all Harley's years with the Bureau, this had to be one of the most concentrated cases she had ever worked, given how much had already happened in just a few days.

As they walked up the hill, Harley waited for Callaway to speak. She knew he had to be struggling with the guilt of knowing he had not stopped the killer, even though he had been waiting at Holy Hope for just that reason. When he did speak, his pained frustration was clear in his voice.

"I can't figure it out. I've been here all night, and not one vehicle has come or gone the whole time."

Even in the pale starlight, Harley could see the weariness on his face. He looked haggard, though she supposed that could have been as much from emotional exhaustion as physical weariness. If the missing woman died, Callaway would probably live the rest of his life believing he could have saved her if only he had been a little more vigilant.

With some agents, Harley might have wondered if they'd actually managed to stay awake the whole time. That was part of the reason for having stakeouts in pairs—they could alternate shifts, one watching while the other slept. But she had no doubt Callaway had remained alert.

"Maybe the killer didn't use the road," she suggested, trying to give him a way out. "Maybe he came from the woods."

"I still would have heard the engine," Callaway answered. "It's been a quiet night, and sound carries a long distance up in these hills."

Harley fell silent. Everything pointed to the killer approaching on foot—assuming he was coming from *outside* the community at all. The more she thought about it, the more convinced she became there was a wolf in sheep's clothing.

Up ahead, several lanterns glowed around a small barn. A number of figures stood near the door, conversing in low voices. The scene was eerie, coming as it did on the heels of the discovery of Isla's and Beverly's bodies earlier that same day.

Unsure how to encourage Callaway, Harley decided to turn the conversation back to the events at hand. "You said only one woman went missing?"

Callaway said nothing for a few moments. Harley supposed he was still trying to puzzle out how the killer had struck without Callaway's knowing.

"It doesn't fit the MO," she continued, trying to pull him out of his thoughts. "He's been attacking pairs until now."

"Oh, it's the same MO," he finally answered. "He just didn't succeed this time."

This caught her attention. "What do you mean?"

"I mean he attacked two, but one got away. She was found by her eight-year-old son—he woke in the middle of the night with a bad dream, and when he couldn't find her in the house, he came out here."

"Nothing like discovering reality is worse than your nightmare," Harley murmured.

Callaway nodded. "Anyway, she's on her way to the hospital now. It appears she was struck from behind. Then, while her attacker busied himself with her friend, she crawled into the hay and hid. That was where her son found her."

"I take it the killer got away with the friend?"

Callaway nodded grimly. "The two just vanished. No footprints, no witnesses. The police are casing the area for any signs of a vehicle, but don't hold your breath. This guy's a ghost."

Harley could feel the stares of the community members. Their voices had died to a low murmur at the approach of the agents, like the distant sound of a brook, so subtle as to be mistaken for the wind.

"Why didn't you call me when it happened?" she said, feeling as if she had been kept out of the loop.

"I did. Call went straight to voicemail."

She couldn't blame him for that.

"Walk me through it?" she said to Callaway, eager to escape the stares of the onlookers.

Callaway reached between the pair of large, rolling doors and pushed one of them open. The wheels overhead gave a faint squeal in protest.

It was a small barn with four stalls, two on each side. At the far end, a matching pair of rolling doors – both open – led out to a pasture of stunted grass. There was a space to the left and right before the stalls began. On the right was a tack room lined with saddles, bridles, helmets, and other riding gear, while to the left was an open room occupied by hand tools, several cracked water buckets, a bin full of twine, and a heap of loose hay.

Callaway redirected Harley's attention to the open doors at the end of the building. "The son claims that the missing woman, Maddie Walsh, was helping his mother, Carol O'Brien, bring the horses in for the night. Normally the horses would stay out, but what with all the killings, Carol wanted to keep a close eye on the animals. Told the kid to get in bed, and she'd read him one of his favorite Russian folk tales when she got back."

"Little did she know she was putting her own life and Maddie's in danger," Harley observed. "Then again, the killer could just as easily have gotten to them another way. We've seen how capable he is."

"I guess it depends on whether he was targeting them or just being opportunistic," Callaway answered. Then, before Harley could give her opinion on this, he turned and pointed to the bin of twine, his wedding band giving a faint wink of light in the glow of the hanging lantern.

"It looks like Carol was bringing the twine back here when she was struck from behind," he continued.

Harley touched one of the frayed ends of rough twine that coiled out from the bin like springs.

"They use it for all kinds of things around here," Callaway explained. "Sandals, ropes, and so on. If nothing else, they can burn it. When you're living off the grid, you learn not to waste anything."

Harley did not answer. Dropping the twine, she drifted down the length of the barn, peering in each stall at the horses quietly pulling stalks of hay from their feed bags. Then her attention rose to the overhead loft, which was mostly empty except for a few rows of hay

111

bales, leftovers from the last cutting.

One of the horses dunked a mouthful of hay into a bucket of water and brought it out, leaving a stream of water on the rubber mats. Another horse kicked the wall.

"Perfect place to ambush someone," Harley mused. "Plenty of distracting sounds."

Callaway watched her silently, his arms crossed as he leaned against one of the stall doors. He looked very much like a cowboy, with his belt buckle and Stetson perched back on his head—a rugged cowboy, not the kind who wore spurs and a bolo tie as a fashion statement. He showed no inclination to rush her.

Harley reached the open doors and peered out into the starlit darkness. The earth was patterned with the crescent marks of the horses' shoes. The ground was mostly flat for half a mile or so before rising up toward the hills, and somewhere out there was a fence line Harley could not see.

Where are you? she thought. *Where have you taken Maddie, and what do you mean to do with her?*

Looping back through the barn, she returned to the place where Carol had been ambushed and studied the shadows along the edge of the wall. Then, on instinct, she turned her flashlight on and stooped, examining the scuff marks made in the dust.

"Did you see these prints?" she said, squatting down. "Looks like he stood here along the wall and waited for her. Might have come in while the women were out wrangling the horses."

A low drumbeat of excitement began to pound in her chest. She might very well be staring at the footprints of the man who had killed four women – six, if she assumed the Rasco sisters were dead – and kidnapped another.

She photographed the prints, then turned to Callaway. He seemed to read her thoughts.

"Don't worry," he said. "I made sure everyone stayed outside. At the rate he's going, though, it might not matter how well we preserve the crime scene. He's dropping bodies more quickly than we can examine them."

Harley took a deep breath, sobered by this reminder. "You're forgetting one key detail," she answered.

Callaway raised an eyebrow.

Harley straightened. "He made a mistake this time—a big one. He left a witness."

She felt an urge to race to the hospital as soon as possible to question their witness. Carol might have seen the suspect and be able to provide a sketch of him, which they could then run against the Bureau's criminal database. If they matched the two, they would have the killer's identity—and a chance of rescuing Maddie.

Callaway, however, did not appear quite so enthusiastic. "Slow your roll," he cautioned. "We need to be thorough here, make sure we have all the facts straight. Besides, she's not even awake yet. She passed out on the stretcher. They'll call when she's awake."

Much as it frustrated her, Harley knew he was right. If they went off half-cocked, they were as likely to make things worse as they were to make them better. Still, waiting didn't sit right with her, not when she knew an innocent woman was in the killer's hands. It never had before, and it didn't now.

"You never told me how you did," Callaway said.

She looked at him blankly.

"At the station?" he prompted. "Looking into missing persons cases?"

"Oh, that." It seemed a lifetime ago that she had searched through the records at the sheriff's department, even though it couldn't have been more than a few hours. "I might have connected our killer to two more murders."

He nodded, looking intrigued. "I'll bite. Go on."

"Two sisters, Beatrice and Bella Rasco, went missing from a farmhouse just down the road from where Sienna and Eleanor lived. Haven't been seen or heard from since. No postcards, no letters, no credit card purchases, nothing."

"You think they might have been the killer's first victims?"

"It's a working theory. Not many pairs of women go missing together."

He nodded, growing contemplative. Harley sensed he was sinking into himself again, and she felt it was her responsibility to keep him optimistic and focused. It would do no good to anybody for him to torture himself with guilt.

She cleared her throat. "We should probably go out and see what these people can tell us about the missing woman."

"It's a waste of time," a voice said.

Harley turned to see Jedediah Landon standing in front of one of the stalls, reaching through the bars to scratch the forehead of the young palomino on the other side. Harley hadn't seen or heard him come in.

"This area's part of an active investigation," Callaway said.

"You're not supposed to be in here."

Harley held up her hand in a calming gesture. "It's okay. Maybe he knows something." She studied Landon. "What do you mean, a waste of time?"

Landon shrugged. "Talking to them. They've had it with you Feds. You can't protect us, can't catch the killer. As far as Gardenia's concerned, you're just…irrelevant."

Gardenia, Harley thought. *Of course she'd think that.*

"You want to help us out?" Callaway said, an edge in his voice. "We'd have a much better chance of catching this guy if your people worked with us instead of against us."

Landon grunted. "You had your chance, and you lost it."

"How's that?" Harley countered. "By not immediately identifying the killer just as soon as someone lent a helping hand? I'm starting to wonder whether you people really want us to put this guy away."

Landon pulled his arm out of the stall and turned toward the agents, his eyes narrowing. "What are you suggesting? You think we're hiding something, like maybe the killer's one of us?"

She waited, not backing down.

Landon laughed in a dismissive, humorless way. "Trust me, if he was one of us, we'd know."

"And what would you do, if you found out he was one of you?"

"I can tell you this much. We wouldn't call you guys."

Callaway stepped in before Harley could reply. "Alright, Landon. We don't need you here to tell us all the things we're doing wrong. If you have information to share, now's your time to tell us. Otherwise…" He cocked his thumb and made a jabbing motion over his shoulder.

Landon stared back, looking defiant for a few moments. Then he sighed, and his stubbornness seemed to blow out with the air.

"Look, you need to find her, alright?" he said, a note of earnestness entering his voice. "We can't lose her, too. It would be too much for all of us."

Harley glanced at Callaway. His expression remained stoic, a perfect poker face.

"What are you talking about?" he said.

Landon tipped his head back and stared up at the ceiling, as if he might find the answer up there. "Maddie was one of the good ones. Everybody respected her. She was this bigshot lawyer, and she left a six-figure career to come way out here and live like a primitive. Sold her house, gave all the money to charity. She was an inspiration to a lot of us, especially the younger girls."

He paused. Harley resisted the urge to pressure him to continue.

"A lot of us are here because we couldn't hack it in the real world," he went on. "We needed an escape. But not Maddie. She could make it anywhere she went."

"So why'd she come to Holy Hope?" Callaway said.

Landon shrugged. "Just got tired of the rat race. Didn't buy into all the commercials and consumerism propaganda. She's a free thinker—and a smart one, too."

Callaway's phone vibrated, and he pulled it out to read a text message.

Landon watched Harley, his eyes pleading with her. "I guess what I'm saying," he continued, "is we need Maddie. Her being here? It gives people hope."

Harley wanted to lean into this, ask him to clarify, but Callaway spoke first.

"Our witness is awake," he said. "We'd better go find out what else she knows."

Harley nodded. Then, turning to Landon, she said, "We'll find Maddie. Whatever it takes, we'll find her."

She didn't know whether they would find her alive or not, and she wondered if Landon would notice the omission. If he did, he didn't comment on it.

"Thank you," he said, nodding solemnly. "And when you do find him, do me one last favor?"

Harley waited.

"Don't bring him back alive," he finished.

CHAPTER TWENTY ONE

Harley woke from a dream and shifted her back, trying to get comfortable on the couch of the Trinity Hospital waiting room. The stiff metal frame just beneath the surface of the upholstery made this nearly impossible, however. It was like snuggling with a skeleton wrapped in a blanket.

"You haven't slept a wink, have you?" she said to Callaway, who sat rigid beside her, his face vacant as he stared at the double doors. They had been waiting for several hours now for Carol O'Brien to wake up, long enough for the glow of daylight to wash in through the windows, but the haggard look on Callaway's face suggested he'd maintained his vigil all night. Harley was beginning to worry about him.

"There was nothing you could have done," she said, hoping to encourage him. "We should have had a whole team watching that community, not just one person. You're not Superman."

Callaway said nothing. It was as if he was encased in a transparent box of soundproof glass.

Harley decided to share something that had been rattling in her head recently.

"I can't help wondering if it's an inside job," she said.

Callaway blinked, but otherwise his face showed no reaction. "What do you mean?"

"Think about it," she continued, turning her body to face him. "An off-grid community, separate from police, from technology. No cameras, no cell phones. You can show up with a criminal record, change your name, and just like that you're a new person. Nobody bats an eye."

Callaway's eyebrows pinched together doubtfully. "So you think one of the community members is the killer? That's a tall task, killing four women right under everyone's noses. The thing about living in a small community is everyone knows everyone else's secrets."

"What if they're protecting the killer because he's one of their own?" She was not sure she bought this theory – it was hard to imagine what the members of Holy Hope would get out of protecting the man who was victimizing them – but she wanted to hear Callaway's

116

reaction. Sometimes you just had to throw theories against the wall and see what stuck.

"Why would they protect someone who's preying on them?" Callaway said, his eyes still on the door.

"Maybe they think he can change, turn over a new leaf. Or maybe it's about the victims. They could be...blacklisted somehow." She knew she was making baseless suggestions, but she wanted to keep Callaway engaged, even if all he did was shoot down her theories. His silence unsettled her more than his anger ever had.

Before he could reply, however, the door opened and a stout nurse in blue scrubs strode through. Her square jaw and arched eyebrows gave her a look of unalterable purpose, like a schoolteacher who won't tolerate one more interruption from the class. She gave the agents a quick once-over. She didn't seem impressed by what she saw.

"Well, she's awake," the nurse said, sounding reluctant to share the news.

Callaway rose half a second before Harley did. As they approached, however, the nurse held up a hand to stop them.

"It's not our policy to let our patients be interrogated," she said, "especially after something like what Ms. O'Brien went through."

"We just need to ask her a few questions," Harley assured her. It was a line she had used countless times before, and it usually worked because it was so reasonable. Who couldn't spare a few minutes to answer a few simple questions, especially if the answers might help stop a murderer?

The nurse, however, crossed her arms and leaned back, eyeing her skeptically. "Do you have any idea what she's been through?"

"Actually, that's why we're—"

"She took a severe blow to the back of her head," the nurse went on, as if Harley hadn't spoken. "At this point, it's not even clear if she could hold an intelligent conversation about the weather, never mind a grueling interrogation by two federal officers."

"Grueling?" Harley repeated, baffled by the nurse's hostility.

Once again, the nurse ignored her. "I've seen how this plays out. You come in here and put the patient through the ringer, not caring what it'll cost them as long as it helps you get the person you're after. But I'm not going to stand for that."

Harley could not believe what she was hearing. She understood a nurse's commitment to caring for the welfare of her patients, but this was simply belligerent. Before she could respond, however, she felt Callaway's hand on her arm, cautioning her.

"I hear you," he said, his voice good-natured and reasonable. "The last thing Carol needs is for us to go in there and ask her to jump through a number of mental hurdles when what she really needs is rest."

The nurse's icy exterior thawed just a little.

"If it was up to me," Callaway said with a soft laugh, "we'd give her a few days of quiet before so much as asking her what year it is."

He shook his head, as if forced to accept the inherent unfairness of life. "But unfortunately – and I'm not sure if you're aware of this – but the man who attacked her also kidnapped her friend. We believe this is the same man who has killed as many as six other women."

The nurse's face grew alarmed. "My God," she murmured, glancing toward the exit. "Do you think he'd come here to finish the job? Is that why there's an officer in the hallway?"

"It's unlikely," Harley said, rejoining the conversation. "The chance that he'll harm Carol's friend, on the other hand..." She trailed off, leaving an ominous silence.

The nurse began to bite her lip as she stared at the floor.

"Frankly," Callaway said, "we can't do this without Carol's help. The longer we wait, the more danger everyone is in—Carol, her friend, any other women the killer might have his eye on. Until he's put away, no one is safe."

Having made his best pitch, Callaway fell silent. Both agents stared at the nurse, who continued to work at her lip. The intercom came alive in the background, paging a doctor.

"Okay," she finally said. "I guess I didn't realize how important this was." Then she raised a warning finger. "But I must insist you keep the conversation to a minimum—five minutes at the most."

"No problem," Callaway answered immediately. "I can't tell you how much of a help this is. I'll be sure to mention it when I file the report."

A flush of red crept into the nurse's cheeks. She cleared her throat and turned abruptly away, pushing through the double doors.

"Well done," Harley murmured softly to Callaway.

Callaway, however, showed no signs of gloating. His face was grim as he moved forward, following the nurse.

As they walked down the bleached-white hallway, Harley couldn't help thinking of her father, who she had visited in a nearby hospital not so long ago. She wondered how he was doing. She didn't like how their last phone conversation had ended: the passive-aggressive way he had insisted he didn't want to inconvenience her, clearly implying she considered her job more important than time with her dying father. It was an unfair suggestion – he had been the one to cancel their lunch appointment, after all – and it rankled Harley that he could be so quick to throw a wrench in the works just when it seemed things were going well after so many years of misunderstanding and frustration.

If he thinks I don't want to see him, she thought, *I'll just have to prove him wrong. Maybe I should just show up, not bother waiting for an invitation. He can't kick me out, can he?*

She was still thinking about her father when the nurse opened the door to Room 405 and ushered her and Callaway inside. Carol O'Brien was sitting up in bed, picking at a cluster of grapes on her tray. A napkin lay crumpled to the side, next to a yogurt cup that looked to have been licked clean.

"Morning, Carol," the nurse said in a matronly voice. "I've brought you some visitors."

A look of apprehension stole across Carol's features when she saw the two agents. Her hands went rigid, her nostrils dilating.

"If you don't want to talk, I can send them out right now," the nurse said quickly, stepping toward the agents as if to shoo them away.

For a moment, Harley thought they'd be unable to talk with Carol, after all. They couldn't force her to do anything, so if she decided to take a firm stance against law enforcement, as Melissa Hargrave had, they would be out of luck. They could convince a judge to issue a subpoena, but that would cost precious time they didn't have.

Then Carol's gaze fixed on Callaway. "Wait…you were at the barn, weren't you? I think I saw you before I passed out."

"That's right," he answered.

Carol gave the nurse a tentative smile. "I'll be alright." Then she returned her attention to Callaway. "I'll answer as many questions as you want, if it'll help you find Maddie."

The nurse smiled indulgently, as if dealing with a well-intentioned but misguided child. "Let's not go overboard, Carol. You need your rest. I'll come back in a few minutes, and if the agents have any further questions, they can stop by tomorrow." She scooped up the food tray. Carol reached for the grapes, but the tray disappeared before she could grab them.

As the door closed behind the nurse, Carol let out a deep sigh. "She means well. She just doesn't want me straining myself."

Harley pulled a chair close to the side of the bed. "We understand," she replied as she sat down. "We just want to find Maddie and stop the man who's doing this."

She pulled out her phone and navigated to her notes. Behind her, Callaway wandered over to the window and peeked through the curtains, giving her space to question the witness—and providing himself a chance to brood over his guilt, no doubt.

"Now," Harley said, offering Carol a gentle smile. "What can you tell us about the attack, Ms. O'Brien?"

Carol lay her head back and stared up at the ceiling, a thoughtful expression on her face. "I've been thinking about it all night, awake and sleeping. It creeps up on me in flashes, like my mind has to keep going over it because it can't accept what happened."

She sat up and looked at Harley. "Does that make sense?"

"Very much so," Harley answered. She waited, not wishing to pressure Carol. In her head, however, she heard the steady ticking of a clock.

Satisfied, Carol lay back down and continued. "It was dark, I remember that much. Maddie and I had just brought the horses in for the night, and we were feeding them—just to keep them occupied overnight, you know."

"Sure."

"Anyway, Maddie knew I was worried about the horses. They're my babies, you understand, and with all the murders around the community, I just felt there was no telling what might happen next. Maddie made a joke about one of the mares who's in heat, and I laughed. She had a good sense of humor."

She paused. Harley wondered if Carol realized she had referred to Maddie in the past tense, as if she were already dead.

"Anyway," Carol continued, "I moved away to throw the twine strings aside—a horse can have all kinds of problems if it eats one of those, so you have to be really careful you pull them out of the bales. Besides, they're useful for all kinds of things: making rope, sandals, ornaments, stuff like that. That's how it goes at Holy Hope: waste not, want not."

Harley nodded politely, trying not to look at the clock hanging on the wall. Footsteps approached down the hall, and Harley stiffened, thinking it might be the nurse returning to chase them out. Then the footsteps went on, and Harley relaxed.

"Is that when you were attacked?" Callaway said, getting the conversation back on the rails. He stepped around the foot of the bed so that he was in Carol's line of sight.

Carol reached back to touch the bandage on her head. "He must've been hiding in the shadows. Next thing I knew, my cheek was pressed to the floor and all I could hear was a rushing of blood in my head. The room was spinning, so I stayed where I was. When I looked up, he was…he was…"

She paused, her jaw trembling. Her eyes darted rapidly side to side.

"It's okay," Harley said, touching Carol's hand. "You're safe now."

"But Maddie isn't," Carol answered, and Harley regretted her words. "He dragged her out like she was a bag of grain. She wasn't fighting or screaming or anything, so she must have been unconscious."

Harley leaned forward intently. "Did you get a good look at him?"

Carol frowned. "It was just so…dark. He was twisted away, looking behind him." She gave a defeated shrug. "There wasn't much to see."

"What about his clothes?" Harley pressed, desperate for even the smallest detail. "Did you notice what he was wearing?"

Carol shook her head.

"Or the way he walked?" Callaway suggested. "Was his back straight?"

"What about his height?" Harley said.

Carol covered her face, overwhelmed. "I don't know, I don't know! It was all so fast, and the barn was so dark. I wish I could describe him for you, but I just can't, okay? I can't."

Harley tried not to let her disappointment show. Carol was the first person they had talked with who claimed to have seen the killer, but she didn't seem to remember anything she'd seen. She might remember more under hypnosis, but that would take far more time than they had today. Besides, she wasn't trained in hypnotic techniques, and as far as she knew, Callaway wasn't either.

"So he dragged Maddie out," Callaway prompted gently. "What happened next?"

"Well," Carol continued with a shaky breath, "I had a feeling he was coming back for me, so I crawled into the pile of loose hay and hid myself. It was the best I could do, given how dizzy I was feeling."

Harley was taking notes on her phone. "Did he come looking for you?" she said without looking up.

"He didn't even make a sound," Carol answered. "Not until he started talking, I mean. He was cursing under his breath, like he was furious he couldn't find me."

"What did he say?" Callaway said.

"'How could you let her go,' 'What's wrong with you,' that kind of thing. He called himself a 'dirty little skink.'"

Harley glanced up, puzzled. "He said what?"

"It's a tiny lizard," Callaway explained.

"Yes, I know what a skink is, thank you. I used to live here."

Callaway raised both hands in self-defense.

Harley turned back to Carol. "Would you recognize his voice if you heard it?"

Carol considered. "I think so. But the way he was talking—it was just so strange. Like he was...growling, almost. A low muttering sound." She shivered.

Harley stared thoughtfully at her notes. The 'skink' bit had caught her by surprise. Was it possible Carol had misheard him? Might he actually have said something like, 'Why don't you ever think?'

Before Harley could voice her thoughts, Callaway altered the line of inquiry.

"Can you think of anyone who might want to harm you or Maddie?" he said.

Carol shook her head without hesitation. "I don't think so. We get along with everybody. We—" Then she paused abruptly, as if a new thought had occurred to her.

"What is it?" Harley said.

"You know Joseph, don't you?"

The two agents exchanged a glance.

"Can't say we've had the pleasure," Callaway answered. "Who is he?"

"I'm surprised you've been to Holy Hope so many times and haven't met him," she continued, looking puzzled. "He's...kind of a big deal. He's the one who leads all the meetings, so I guess you could say he's more or less in charge."

"I thought Ms. Hargrave was calling the shots," Harley said.

Carol shook her head. "Gardenia takes care of the day-to-day details. She's the practical one: detail-oriented, hard-working to a fault. But Joseph..." She paused, pursing her lips. "Joseph's the spiritual leader. A real visionary. He lets Gardenia make the little decisions, but when it comes to something serious, Joseph has the final say."

"Are they...together?" Callaway ventured.

A soft laugh escaped Carol. "Joseph and Gardenia? No. Suffice to say, Gardenia's not his type."

Harley raised an eyebrow, wondering what this meant. She made a note of it but did not interrupt Carol. They had bigger fish to fry.

"Anyway," Carol continued, "some people saw Maddie as a threat to Joseph. She called him out, questioned his decisions, something Gardenia never does. There were those – myself included – who wondered what the community might look like under Maddie's leadership."

Harley's pulse quickened. Finally, a motive for the attack.

"You think Joseph might want to silence her?" she said. "What about the other victims—why would he harm them?"

Carol frowned thoughtfully, considering the question. As she took a breath to answer, however, the door opened and the nurse came in. The nurse smiled at Carol, then gave the agents a severe look.

"I think you've gone well over your five minutes, don't you?" she said coldly.

Harley rose. "Thank you for your help, Carol. If you think of anything else—"

"She'll be sure to let you know," the nurse interrupted, holding the door open. "But right now, all she needs to think about is getting the rest she needs."

Realizing there was no point arguing, the two agents stepped out into the hallway. The door closed behind them with a loud clap of finality. Harley couldn't help wondering what crucial details they might have learned had they been allowed to stay a little longer.

As they walked down the hallway, Callaway brushed his knuckles against the side of his jaw. "All the time we've spent at Holy Hope," he said, "and nobody's mentioned this Joseph character to us until now?"

It struck Harley as odd, too. How had they not bumped into him or at least heard his name used? Harley had gotten the impression from Ms. Hargrave that she was the one who got things done at Holy Hope, but according to Carol, there was someone with even more say than she had.

The question was, why did he stay behind the scenes?

She thought of the earlier theory she had proposed about the killings being an inside job. It didn't sound quite so outlandish now.

"If he's involved," she suggested, "they could be protecting him."

"That theory still doesn't hold water to me," Callaway answered as he pushed open a door and stepped back into the waiting room. "You don't nurture a parasite—you cut it out."

"Unless they don't know what he's up to."

Callaway stopped and frowned at her.

"Remember what Landon said?" she continued. "A lot of people at the community have criminal backgrounds. By keeping his existence a secret, they might think they're keeping him from being persecuted for old crimes that have no relevance any more. They think we're incompetent and ineffectual, so it probably wouldn't be a hard sell."

"And their silence helps him cover up new crimes."

"Exactly."

Callaway considered this for a few moments. Then he shrugged. "We won't know one way or the other till we talk to him. But to do that, we need to find him. If we have to turn that community upside down to do it, so be it."

"There might be another way," Harley suggested, fishing her phone from her pocket. She dialed a number and held it a few inches from her ear while it rang.

"After last night's attack," she explained to Callaway, "the sheriff sent a few cars over there to keep watch. They might be able to tell us if Joseph is there."

After a few moments, the gravelly voice of Sheriff Santiago answered.

"What can I do for you, Harley?"

"Do you know a Joseph over at Holy Hope by any chance? I'm told he's their 'spiritual leader.'"

The sheriff was silent for a few heartbeats.

"Warren, right? He's that religious nut, isn't he?" Santiago finally said.

Harley glanced at Callaway. The phone wasn't on speaker, but the volume was high enough that Callaway could probably hear every word.

"Possibly so," Harley answered. "We think he might have attacked those two women last night, and we're trying to locate him. I figured you could check with your guys over at the community and ask if they've seen him."

The sheriff cleared his throat. Harley heard the rustling of paper.

"Actually," he answered, "he left the community about an hour ago. My boys have been keeping track of everyone who comes and goes. Those Luddites might not like it, but we're just trying to catch a killer, same as they are."

Harley's heart sank. If Warren knew they were on to him, he could be in the wind. It took less than four hours to reach the Mexican border, which meant that if Warren was thinking of leaving the country, he would have a significant head start.

"Did he say where he was going?" Harley said, not really expecting to learn anything useful.

"He did, surprisingly enough," the sheriff answered, sounding surprised himself. "Claimed he was on his way to an auction at a small mine nearby. It's called...let's see..."

There was that sound of rustling paper again. "The Joya del Sur," he finished.

"I didn't know the community was into buying mines," Harley murmured.

"Usually they're not, but they have a few investment properties in the area that keep them afloat—a condo, a couple of office buildings they rent out, that kind of thing."

"Very progressive of them."

Santiago laughed. "There's no such thing as true isolation, not in the twenty-first century."

Harley grew thoughtful. "Well, thank you for the help."

"Always a pleasure."

"Joya del Sur," Callaway repeated as Harley hung up the phone. "I think I know where it is. Come on, let's go pay him a visit." He started moving toward the parking lot. Harley, however, stayed where she was.

"We should split up," she said.

He looked puzzled. "What are you talking about?"

"We have no idea where Maddie is."

"And that's why we need to get Warren talking," Callaway interrupted.

Harley shook her head, frustrated. "For all we know, she could be back at Holy Hope, locked in Warren's closet. We need to cover as much ground as possible."

Callaway took a step toward her, his hands held up in a pleading gesture. "Harley, this guy could be a serial killer. Do you have any idea how dangerous he could be?"

"More than you do," Harley answered, holding her ground. "I'm sorry to pull rank on you, but I have a lot more experience with serials than you do."

Callaway dropped his hands. He didn't look happy. "You want to split up? Fine. I'll go after Warren, you go to Holy Hope. That's the only way we're doing this."

Harley took a deep breath, trying not to grow exasperated. "If I go back to Holy Hope, Ms. Hargrave – Gardenia, or whatever she's calling herself today – will strangle me with her own bare hands. Or I'll strangle her, one or the other."

Callaway made a sound that was half grunt, half laugh.

"You're better with the locals, remember?" she continued. "I need you to trust me on this."

He stared at her for several long seconds. Then he shook his head reluctantly, as if he knew he would later regret his decision.

"Okay," he answered, "we'll do it your way." Then he held up a finger. "But the moment things get dicey, you call for backup, understand?"

"Yes, sir."

He gave her another long look to make it clear he didn't like this plan. He sighed. "Just be careful, okay?"

"You, too. There's more going on in that community than meets the eye."

As they went their separate ways in the parking lot, Harley thought about Maddie out there in the killer's clutches. She hoped it was not too late to save her.

CHAPTER TWENTY TWO

Harley smiled at the security guard as he leaned over his clipboard, scanning the list of names written there. She maintained a calm exterior from the seat of her Jeep, but inwardly she was wondering how in the world she was going to convince this man to let her into Joya del Sur.

It would have been easy enough to flash her badge, tell the young man with the military haircut and straining biceps the true nature of her visit, and be on her way. But she suspected the guard might tip off his employer to the arrival of an FBI agent, and the employer in turn might do something that would spook Warren before Harley could surprise him. If Warren was indeed the serial killer they were after, he would be on high alert, knowing the police might come looking for him at any moment.

This might be their only shot at bringing him in.

The guard hummed as he ran his finger down the list. When he reached the end, he made a soft clucking sound.

"Doesn't look like I've got you," he said, glancing up. The green of his eyes was striking against the coffee brown of his skin.

"Really?" Harley replied, frowning as if she could not make sense of this. "I was sure he set it up. You checked his name, too? Gregory Cole?"

As the guard checked the list again, Harley stared down the dirt path that ran along the edge of the open copper pit, a crater so massive that it brought Harley back to the last time she had visited the Grand Canyon. Shelves of blasted rock descended into the pit like stairs toward a floor too deep for Harley to glimpse. At the top of the stairs, a straight shot from where Harley was parked beside the security booth, was a long warehouse with a number of buildings parked out front, one of which probably belonged to Joseph Warren.

She imagined herself shifting into drive and gunning the engine, ignoring the shouts of the security guard behind her. She would fish-tail to a stop, race into the warehouse, and a few minutes later she'd be coming out with Warren in handcuffs—*if* everything went her way. But it was a big *if.*

And what if Warren is armed? she thought. *What if he starts shooting or takes a hostage?*

"I'm sorry," the guard said, setting the clipboard aside. "No dice."

He glanced to his right as a vehicle came up behind Harley. She realized her time was limited. If she didn't convince him soon, he was going to get suspicious, and that wouldn't make her job any easier.

"He must have simply forgotten," she said with a pleasant smile. "He has some savings, you see, but he just doesn't have time to research ways to invest it. I offered to help, and...well..." She shrugged. "Here I am."

"I'm sorry, ma'am, but my employer doesn't want anyone coming in who isn't serious about investing in his company. I can't let you in just to observe."

The car behind them gave an impatient little honk. The guard held up a hand, gesturing for them to wait.

Seeing no other options, Harley decided to level with him. She leaned close and spoke in a low, confidential voice.

"Okay. You want the truth? I'm with the FBI, and I'm looking for a potential suspect." She held up her badge, being careful to keep it hidden from the view of the vehicle behind her.

The security guard studied the badge carefully, as if worried it might be a fake. His brow furrowed.

"But you can't let anyone know why I'm here," Harley added, returning the badge to her belt. "If you do, the suspect might run—and that would be grounds to press charges against you."

The guard looked unimpressed. "No need to make threats. I served three tours in Iraq—I know how to run an op. What'd this guy do?"

"Multiple homicides. Allegedly."

The man nodded stoically, his face betraying no surprise. "Okay, here's the deal. You're now..." He consulted his clipboard. "Veronica Banks. She's a no-show, and the auction's about to start."

"Sure she's not behind me?"

"Not unless Veronica is sporting a toupee. And if she does show up late, I'll just say you lied to me and I forgot to check your license because you were batting your eyelashes at me."

Harley couldn't help smiling. She decided she liked this security guard.

"Thank you for the help," she said.

"Don't mention it. Happy hunting."

Harley drove through, feeling a flush of warmth in her cheeks from the stranger's compliment. She had caught a lucky break. Now all she had to do was find Warren.

As she parked her car, a group of figures in hard hats stepped out of the warehouse. The man at the front was tall and clean-shaven, and wore a pinstripe suit—the owner of the operation, Harley guessed. Beside him walked a short, heavyset man with a grizzled beard and an orange safety jacket over his sleeveless t-shirt. The foreman, probably. Then came a score or so of potential investors, some on their phones, others murmuring together in low voices as the man at the helm spoke in glowing terms about the output of the mine.

"You all have the quarterly reports," he said, leading the group along the edge of the pit. "I think you'll see our growth is trending in the right direction. We're on track to double our production in just two years."

At the tail of the group, surrounded by three burly men in suits, was a white-robed figure with a curly beard falling halfway down his chest. His face wore a serene expression, and his eyes seemed to dance with an inner mirth, as if he were in on some private joke to which the rest of the world was not privy.

Staring at the man who was undoubtedly Joseph Warren, Harley felt certain she had seen him before. But where, and when?

"As you'll see in the packet you each received," the man in the pinstripe suit continued, "this is the perfect time to invest in copper, which has been steadily rising in value the past few years. Experts predict that by 2030…"

Harley tuned out the man's voice as she exited the vehicle and began shadowing the group. She slipped on a pair of sunglasses so she could study Warren without being quite as obvious, and she couldn't help noticing how little interest he showed in what was going on around him. When the owner pointed to a particular piece of heavy machinery, for instance, Harley caught Warren facing the opposite direction as he watched a passing butterfly. At other times he inspected his nails or kicked at the dirt like a bored child.

You might dissociate, too, if you'd just killed four people in the last few days, Harley reminded herself.

As they moved away from the edge of the pit, Harley decided it was time to act. Just as she approached Warren, however, her phone rang. She considered ignoring it, but then she saw Callaway's name.

Harley turned to the side, trying to act like she hadn't just been making a beeline toward Warren. She held the phone to her ear. "What is it?" she whispered, annoyed.

"Someone woke up on the wrong side of the bed," Callaway answered, unperturbed.

"Someone didn't sleep last night. What do you need, Callaway? I'm in the middle of something here."

"You'll want to hear what I'm about to say." He paused, drawing out the suspense. "One of Maddie's neighbors had a camera."

"A camera?" Harley repeated, puzzled at the thought of anyone keeping that kind of modern technology at a place like Holy Hope. "But isn't that—"

"Against the rules, right." Callaway chuckled. "Apparently, though, there were some break-ins a while back, so they installed a camera without telling anyone. I never would have found out if I hadn't gone door-to-door. Gardenia's not happy, but she'll survive."

"What did they steal, straw hats?"

"Try jewelry. Apparently the deal is you leave everything from your old life behind when you enter the community, but it doesn't always happen that way in practice. Behind the charming facade, this place is chock full of secrets."

"Clearly," Harley murmured, watching as the group returned to the edge of the pit. Warren hung back a few paces, picking at something on his robe.

"So what did this camera show?" Harley said.

"You ready for this?"

"You know I hate it when you keep me in suspense."

"We've got our very own Joseph Warren creeping into Maddie's house just last night."

A shiver went down Harley's spine. "You're kidding."

"I promise you I'm not."

"Any idea what he was doing?"

"Looking for Maddie, I imagine. When he didn't find her there, he went over to the barn. I think you can guess what happened next."

It was a good lead, and Harley knew they'd been lucky to learn about the camera. One thing troubled her, however.

"What about Carol, though?" she said. "If he was focused on Maddie, why'd he attack Carol? To get her out of the way? She made it sound like her attacker was upset he couldn't find her."

"Wouldn't you be upset, too, knowing the only witness to your latest crime was still alive?"

Harley caught the foreman staring at her. He leaned close to his boss and whispered something to him.

"Look," Harley replied to Callaway, "I have to go. I'm going to bring Warren in."

There was a note of concern in Callaway's voice. "Why don't you wait for me to back you up? I can be there in fifteen, twenty minutes."

130

"There isn't time. He could be gone by then. I've got this—trust me."

Callaway sighed. "Okay. I trust you. Just don't make me regret it."

Hanging up the phone, Harley decided she had waited long enough. She needed to strike while she had the opportunity. For all she knew, this might be the best chance she would get.

Warren's back was to Harley as she strode toward him. She had almost reached him when a beefy, sandal-clad man moved between her and Warren, walling him off. Harley could just make out the numbers 211 tattooed along the side of the man's neck—a number used by the Crips, a Los Angeles-based street gang that was one of the most violent in the world. The numbers stood for "BK," or "Blood Killer," indicating the wearer had killed a member of the Crips' rival gang, the Bloods.

This man was no stranger to violence.

"Where the hell do you think you're going?" he said coldly. Behind him, Harley could see three more men watching her with the same dead stare, as if they wouldn't feel the slightest compunction about picking her up and tossing her into the pit.

She noticed the way the gang member in front of her kept his hand close to his pocket. What did he have there, a knife? A gun? Whatever it was, Harley needed to make sure it didn't come out. She needed to de-escalate the situation, find a peaceful solution rather than resorting to violence. She had every right to arrest Warren, but she got the impression these men didn't care much for the law.

"Easy, fellas," she said. "I just need to bring your boss down to the station to ask him a few questions."

The gang member's eyes traveled slowly up and down her body without expression. "What are you, a Fed?"

"That's right," she answered evenly. "I'm investigating the murders at Holy Hope. You might have heard about them."

He snorted. "Some job you've been doing. It's like that saying: 'When seconds count, the police are only minutes away.' How does it feel, being a glorified clean-up crew?"

A younger Harley might have threatened to take them all down to the station. She would have itched for a confrontation, a chance to show she could hold her own. But the years had matured her, and she knew better than to stoop to the level of every thug she crossed, especially ones as dangerous as these.

"Look," she confided, "there are two possibilities here. One, your boss is innocent and this is all just a big misunderstanding. We'll clear things up, and he can go on his merry way. Or two, your boss is a serial killer and needs to be held accountable for his crimes. Do you really want to protect a murderer?"

Harley regretted the words as soon as she spoke them. A man who memorialized his own killing with a tattoo would probably not respond well to an appeal to his conscience.

"You forgot number three," he replied. "He goes to the station and you frame him for something he didn't do. Happens all the time."

"In Hollywood, it does. Not here in New Mexico."

The man grunted. "Says the Fed."

"Is everything alright?" the foreman said, stepping toward them with his hands on his hips. "We've got a schedule here."

"And you can shove it up your ass," the gang member answered, keeping his eyes on Harley.

The foreman stared for a few seconds, then shook his head and walked back to his boss.

"Listen," Harley began. "Warren is going to have to answer some questions, one way or another. He can go in my car, or he can have a police escort. Personally I'd think he'd prefer to avoid the embarrassment."

"Embarrassment?" the gang member repeated. "Like, what? Someone tipping off the media so every local station can send reporters to film the arrest of Joseph Warren, suspected serial killer?"

"That's not going to happen."

"Right. Because he ain't going with you." He shook his head, as if Harley were a lost cause. "What are you trying to do, anyway? He's got the best lawyers money can buy. They'll have him out of there soon as his twenty-four hours are up."

It was always interesting to Harley how familiar the public had become with the rules limiting law enforcement. It was good for citizens to understand the justice system, but sometimes she wished not everyone understood just how little power she sometimes had.

"Maybe so," she answered. "But if you think he'll be able to go back to life as usual after that, you're burying your head in the sand. Even if we can't prove his guilt, that won't mean he's innocent. Reporters will descend on Holy Hope like vultures on a corpse. And who knows what they'll find, if they do enough digging?"

The man gave her a resentful stare. "You just can't leave a good thing alone, can you? You can't be part of it, so you have to find a way to ruin it."

"I'm not the one being stalked by a killer."

They stared at one another. Harley was beginning to regret her decision to turn down Callaway's offer of backup. If she was not careful, things could get ugly in a hurry.

Then Warren spoke up. "Let her through, Marco, let her through." He chuckled apologetically, as if this were all some trivial misunderstanding.

Marco glared at Harley a few moments longer before moving.

"Now," Warren said, clasping his hands together, "what can I do for you, agent?"

Harley pulled out her cuffs. "You can start by showing me your hands. I'm placing you under arrest for suspicion of murder."

A faint look of surprise crossed Warren's face. "Murder?" he repeated. "I have no idea what you're talking about."

"You can tell me all about your innocence when we get to the station."

Taking his arm, she guided it behind his back so she could cuff him. Then she led him away, ignoring the grumbles of his bodyguards. Warren did not say a word as Harley guided him into the back seat of her vehicle.

That went better than I expected, she thought, relieved to no longer have to deal with Warren's henchmen. He could have refused to go with her, told his men to toss her into the pit. Instead he had gone meekly.

Why? Because he was innocent, or because he didn't think they could prove anything?

Troubled, Harley closed Warren's door and moved around to the driver side. As she did so, she glimpsed Warren through the window and felt a chill.

He was smiling.

CHAPTER TWENTY THREE

Harley leaned back in her chair, studying Warren across the table. He hadn't said a word since she'd picked him up, which was odd. Innocent people usually had a hundred questions about why they'd been arrested, and even the guilty ones made a show of having no idea what the police would want with them.

Warren, in contrast, behaved as if he simply didn't care. He folded his hands and rested them on the table, staring back at Harley with a serene expression, his breathing slow and regular, swelling out from his abdomen.

"Mr. Warren, can you tell me where you've been the last two nights?" Harley said, glancing at the one-way mirror as she got started. Callaway was on the other side of the glass, watching the proceedings as he updated Newbury on the case.

Warren tapped his fingers on the edge of the table. "In my home in Holy Hope, of course. I spend every night there. It's a...sacred space, you could say. I'm never away after sunset."

"And you have witnesses who can corroborate that?"

He shrugged. "Nobody watches me sleep, but I'm pretty sure they'd hear me drive off in the middle of the night."

Harley studied him, trying to make sense of his lackadaisical attitude. "Do you know why you're here, Mr. Warren?"

Warren cocked his head at Harley as if the question amused him. "There's a whole host of ways I could answer that," he answered. "Do you mean the question existentially – why was I placed on this earth – or literally—what series of events led me to be sitting in this room? Because the answer is very different depending on the framework of the question."

"I'm asking if you know why we picked you up," she answered.

He smiled and looked down at the table. "In the end, how much can we actually know? Take the Matrix, for example. Can you or anyone else prove we are not in an artificial construct right this moment? Can you really prove to me that anything outside my own existence is real—that you yourself are not a projection of my subconscious mind? If you study epistemology—"

"How about life in prison?" Harley interrupted, losing patience. "Is that real to you? Because that's what you're facing here."

Warren nodded in an indulgent way, as if humoring a child. "You think I'm connected with the killings at Holy Hope. How you reached that conclusion, I cannot imagine, but I give you props for creativity. You are either very imaginative or you've been talking to someone who likes to tell tall tales."

"Actually, we have a witness who doesn't tell tall tales. A witness who tells it like it is, every time."

"A witness?" For the first time, doubt creased Warren's forehead. "What are you talking about, a witness?"

Harley did not reply. With deliberate slowness, she picked up the messenger bag leaning against her chair and set it on the table. She unzipped it. As she pulled the laptop out, Warren's expression changed to curiosity.

He didn't know there was a camera, she thought. That was good. The less Warren knew, the more surprised he would be—and unguarded. With any luck, Harley would pressure him into a mistake before he recovered his poise.

Harley opened the laptop, started the video, and spun the laptop around so Warren could see it. She studied his face, watching for the fleeting micro-expressions that so often gave away a person's true feelings.

Warren leaned forward, an expression of open, childlike interest on his face. "Where'd you get this?" he murmured. "This must be Maddie's house. I didn't think anyone would have had the guts to bring a camera into Holy Hope." He chuckled.

Harley was unsettled by the man's total lack of worry. Even if he was innocent, he had to know the camera footage showed him in a bad light. How was he not concerned?

"Is that you, Mr. Warren?"

Warren shook his head, bemused.

"No?" Harley pressed. "That's not you?"

"No, I mean…" He chuckled softly. "It's me, of course. I just can't believe someone at Holy Hope has such contraband. I knew some of our people took liberties, but this…" He shrugged and shook his head again, as if not sure what to make of it.

Harley was growing annoyed. The interrogator's greatest tool was fear: fear of prison, public humiliation, the unknown. But Warren seemed inexplicably calm.

"Are you high, Mr. Warren?" she said.

"Not in the way you mean, no."

Harley did not take the bait. "Did you or did you not enter Maddie Walsh's home last night?"

He nodded. "I wanted to talk with her."

"About what?"

"Some rumors have been circulating that she's…unhappy with my leadership style. I wanted to talk it over with her one-on-one, nip it in the bud. There is no community without unity."

Harley resisted the urge to roll her eyes. "You couldn't talk with her during the day? It had to be at ten o'clock at night—in the seclusion of her home, no less?"

He shrugged. "The days are long and busy; I had other things going on. Besides, the things we needed to talk about…" He paused, pursing his lips. "They weren't for others to hear. We needed privacy."

"Just what exactly were you planning to talk to her about?"

He smiled. "That, I'm afraid, is not for you to know. Sensitive information, you understand. But I assure you, nothing about it would help you catch your killer—or find Maddie."

He leaned back and stretched his arms behind the chair, yawning. "In any case, this proves nothing. She was taken from the barn, not her house. I never saw her last night."

The door opened and Callaway entered. Harley watched him, unsure what he planned to do.

"You want to know how it looks to me?" Callaway said to Warren without preamble. "You had a problem with Maddie, the kind of problem you couldn't just talk through, and you worried how much she was influencing the others. You worried she was undermining you. How am I doing so far?"

Warren stared at him blankly. The bemused expression, however, was gone—a small victory, but a victory nonetheless.

"So you took matters into your own hands," Callaway continued. "Maybe you weren't sure what you were going to do when you went to her home, but you had to do something, didn't you? She was leading the others away from you, compromising the structure of the community."

Warren's nostrils flared. "Everything she said was a lie."

Callaway placed one hand on the table, the other on the back of Warren's chair. "What lies?" he demanded. "What was she saying?"

Warren looked away and said nothing. After a few moments, Callaway withdrew and began pacing.

"When you couldn't find her at home," he continued, "you might have given up. But you're not the giving up sort, are you? You're

136

persistent, resourceful. So you went to the barn."

"No." Warren's denial was flat, emotionless. Callaway went on as if he hadn't heard.

"When you found her there with Carol, you realized this was the perfect opportunity to rid yourself of a problem—two problems, actually. There's no telling how much Maddie might have poisoned Carol's mind, so why not get rid of her, too?"

"You're wrong."

"Which is what you've been doing all along, isn't it?" Callaway went on, gaining steam. "Ridding yourself of problems. Sienna and Eleanor gave you a bad name by leaving the community, so they had to go. Isla and Beverly—well, we heard the rumors. They weren't exactly following the 'no sex until you're eighteen' rule, were they?"

Warren seemed taken aback. "What rule?"

Callaway paused. "Are you telling me there isn't a rule against minors having sex?"

"There's a rule against dating, sure," Warren agreed. "Dating is a romantic relationship. It takes maturity to grow and maintain a relationship."

"And sex is just, what, a bit of recreational fun?"

Warren smiled patiently. "Sex is bonding. It respects neither age nor prior commitment. That is one of the reasons you have such a violent society: You spend all your time suppressing urges that are perfectly natural, and that frustration manifests itself as social aggression."

It occurred to Harley that this was Warren's defense mechanism: He deflected by making the conversation abstract, philosophical. She needed to keep the conversation concrete. The more personal and relevant, the better.

She thought of what Violet had said about Isla being involved with an older man.

"What was your relationship with Isla and Beverly?" she said.

Warren blinked. "Nothing. I hardly knew them."

The thought of the two victims brought Harley's mind back to the crime scene, and suddenly she knew why Warren looked familiar. He was the man who had seen the two bodies and run away, upset and talking to himself.

"So you weren't sleeping with Isla?" she pressed, wondering if his behavior at the potato field had been a show. "After all, it's just sex."

Warren turned away, disgusted. "You don't have any idea what you're talking about."

Harley went on, certain she had found a weak point. "It must have made you pretty jealous when she and Beverly got involved with Hector Nunez, didn't it?"

"Jealous?" Warren laughed, but there was no humor in the sound. "Of that deadbeat druggie? What on earth could he ever have that I don't already have?"

"Youth. They were drawn to him, weren't they? You might have a silver tongue, sure, and you might be the venerable leader to those at Holy Hope, but at the end of the day you're still an old man—a selfish, creepy, vengeful old man who hides behind—"

"I *fathered* them!" Warren roared, striking the table with his palm. "They had nobody when they came to Holy Hope – *nobody* – and I took them in! *I* took care of them as their own fathers never could, *I* wiped their tears and taught them how to be strong women, *I* prepared them for a future that would actually be worth living!"

"But they never got that future, did they?" Harley answered softly, confident now that she had him on the ropes. "You did all that work preparing them, and then, in a moment's rage, you destroyed it all. It must eat away at you, knowing who they could have become, what they could have done."

Warren clenched his fists as he stared at the floor. "I...did not...kill them."

Harley studied him. She'd thought he was close to cracking, but he still clung to his innocence even after that outburst.

"Then who did?" Harley said, wanting to keep Warren talking.

Warren threw up his hands. "You got me, detective. But I'd be mighty interested to hear once you figure it out."

Harley sat back, feeling suddenly deflated. They had no confession, no hard evidence linking Warren to the crimes, nothing but circumstantial evidence and conjectures. If she didn't get him to say something incriminating, he would walk.

She decided to play her last card.

"I know about the farmhouse," she said.

Warren stared at her blankly.

"The one on Sawyer Pass?" Harley added. "Remember it? Beatrice and Bella Rasco?"

Warren glanced at Callaway, as if confused. "I may have heard the names before, but I don't know what you're getting at."

"What did you do with their bodies?" Harley pressed, not believing his act. "If you show us where they are, we might be able to lighten your sentence."

138

Warren was silent for several moments, staring at her as if he could see right through her.

"No further comment," he said.

The two agents exchanged a glance. Callaway gestured toward the door, and Harley followed him out, feeling suddenly exhausted. They had hit another brick wall.

"We're going to have to let him go," she said as she rubbed her face. Warren hadn't asked for a lawyer, which was good, but that didn't mean he had anything more to say. With or without a lawyer, they would have to charge him or let him go.

"You're getting ahead of yourself," Callaway answered. "We have him on statutory rape, if nothing else."

"Not without a confession or a witness, we don't. It's all hearsay."

Callaway opened his mouth as if to argue, then shut it again. He shook his head, looking disgusted at the prospect of Warren going free.

"I know you don't want to hear this," Harley continued, "but he may have actually cared about those girls in his own twisted way. He may have actually believed he was helping them, filling a role their biological fathers had neglected."

"Fathers aren't supposed to have sex with their children."

"No, they're not."

"So why are you trying to justify him?"

Harley threw up her hands, frustrated. "I'm not justifying him. I'm saying I don't think he would have killed them. He wanted to be their hero, their protector. So why would he murder them in cold blood?"

Callaway was silent.

"Besides," Harley added, "we have no way of connecting him with the first two murders, nor can we explain why he would kill in pairs. We have motive for one murder, not six."

"Doesn't mean he's innocent," Callaway grumbled. But she could see in his eyes that he knew she was right. Unless they could find a way to make the statutory rape charge stick, Warren would be a free man in twenty-four hours.

"What if it's a coincidence?" Callaway suggested. "He takes advantage of the killings to commit a murder of his own?"

"That doesn't explain the other odd details—the muttering, the reference to a skink. By Carol's description, the killer sounds mentally unstable."

"And Warren's not?"

"Not in the way Carol described, no."

Callaway fell silent again. Harley did not like it any more than he did, but there was no use trying to force the evidence to fit their theories.

"I need to go talk to Santiago about that farmhouse," she said. "I can't help thinking it's connected."

"Worth a shot," Callaway answered, but he did not sound optimistic. Harley could tell he was disappointed they weren't in the middle of taping a confession from Warren.

"I'll stay here," he continued. "I'm not letting that man out of my sight until I've crossed every *t* and dotted every *i*. If he wants to lawyer up, fine. But I'm not giving him an out."

Harley couldn't help but admire his tenacity. "Just don't let him get under your skin," she said. "I won't be there to hold you back."

Callaway grunted. "And let him play the innocent suspect roughed up by the corrupt Feds? No thanks."

They both fell silent. Harley could feel the long hours of the case taking their toll on her, pulling her down like a physical weight. But she couldn't take the night off, not when she had no reason to believe the killer was slowing down.

She found Callaway studying her, his forehead creased with concern. "You gonna be alright?"

"Just tired," she answered. "And I have to admit, I was hoping Warren was our guy."

"He still might be. We can't prove it now, but that doesn't mean he's innocent."

She made no reply. She wanted him to be right, because as long as the killer was in custody, the rest of the residents of Holy Hope would be safe.

The evidence, however, did not seem to want to cooperate with them.

"I guess we'll find out soon enough," she answered.

Callaway cocked his head at her, confused. Then understanding dawned in his eyes.

"We'll see if the killer keeps up the pattern and attacks again tonight," he said. "While Warren is behind bars."

Harley nodded. "Exactly. I really hope we got the right guy, because if we didn't, it might not matter how many squad cars we send over to Holy Hope. As long as the killer is on the loose, no one is safe."

CHAPTER TWENTY FOUR

Harley waited in Sheriff Santiago's office, peering through the blinds for Deputy Sonny. She hadn't seen the deputy as she passed his desk, so she thought she was safe. But she couldn't be too careful.

"Looking for someone?" a voice said behind her.

She turned around to see Santiago standing in the doorway, his sleeves rolled up to reveal splashes of muddy water on his forearms. The top two buttons of his uniform were unbuttoned as well, and there was a grayish stain on his right cheekbone.

"What happened to you?" Harley said, surprised by his disheveled appearance.

"Ah, just the usual fun," he answered, plucking a tissue from a box sitting on the shelf beside a framed picture of a boy playing soccer. "Had to serve an eviction notice, and the tenant had gone to town on the building—concrete down the toilet, oven burners on, silverware in the garbage disposal, you name it. I got all this—" He made a vague gesture to indicate the grime on his arms—"fixing a pipe in the basement. Guy went at it with a hammer like it was a pinata."

"I didn't know you were a plumber."

Santiago shrugged as he scrubbed at the gray patches on his arms. "It was my step-father's trade. I could've just waited till they shut off the main, but it's hard to see a problem and not fix it."

"I know the feeling," Harley agreed. That very need – what Rob had referred to as her "savior complex" – had gotten her into trouble more times than she could count. But it was also what kept her working cases long after others had given up.

Santiago crumpled the tissue and tossed it into a nearby trash bin, arching his arm as if taking a free throw. "So," he said, turning back to Harley, "learn anything from your suspect?"

"Sure you don't want to go get washed up? I can wait."

Santiago wrinkled his nose and shook his head, leaning his back against the desk. "A little grime never killed anybody. I want to hear all about this Joseph Warren."

Harley couldn't help appreciating the sheriff's down-to-earth personality, a refreshing contrast to the attitude of some of the officials she had worked with back east, particularly a few bigwigs in the

Bureau. He cared about justice—not politics, not jurisdiction, but putting the bad guys away.

"A little," Harley admitted. "He's tough to read, though. He seems more amused than anything else, as if this is all just a game to him."

"It is, for a lot of them. What do you have on him so far?"

"We've got a video of him entering the home of the missing woman just last night," she answered, deciding this was the strongest piece of evidence against Warren.

"Sounds damning," the sheriff said.

"I thought so, too." She hesitated, her eyes wandering across the spines of the books on Santiago's shelf, hardly seeing them. It would all be much simpler if she could just tell herself Warren was the killer, but she was having trouble connecting the dots.

Santiago unleashed a heavy, sympathetic sigh. "But you're having doubts; is that accurate?"

She nodded, hoping he would help her find some clarity.

"You're making this too complicated, analyzing his behavior," the sheriff said. "You need to get back to the basics. What's the hard evidence? You have the camera footage, which is suspicious but not proof of wrongdoing—nothing beyond breaking and entering, at the worst. How's his alibi?"

"Not much of one. Claims he was alone in his home each of the past few nights. He called it his 'sacred space.' Said he's never away after sunset."

Santiago raised his eyebrows. "Okay. So he's got no alibi. What about motive?"

"The missing woman, Maddie Walsh, seems to have been causing him some trouble. She didn't buy into his religious ideas, and she was vocal in her criticism. He admitted as much."

"So he felt threatened. Sounds like a solid motive to me."

Harley pressed her lips together in a doubtful line. "But what about the other six? And why's he killing in pairs?"

The sheriff frowned as if he had missed something. "Six?"

"I'm counting the two Rasco sisters along with the four confirmed homicides."

The sheriff's troubled expression told Harley she needed to back up and start from the beginning.

"I stopped by yesterday," she began, "to see if any other pairs of women had gone missing in the area, and I came across a report about two women, Beatrice and Bella Rasco, who went missing from their farmhouse out on Sawyer Pass."

Santiago nodded slowly. "Yes, I remember. That was some months ago."

"Six months, in fact. Anyway, I have a theory the sisters were our killer's first victims. I went out to the farmhouse, but it looks like it's been abandoned since the sisters went missing, and it doesn't appear they did much to take care of it when they were still around."

Santiago furrowed his bushy eyebrows. "It's not abandoned."

Harley paused, confused. "What do you mean, not abandoned? I saw the pigs, but I just assumed they were being taken care of by a friendly neighbor. The house is…well…not in the best of shape. Who's living there?"

"The younger brother of the two sisters who went missing. Name's Brandon. I've kept it off the books for tax reasons—the guy is stunted, mentally and emotionally. I always felt bad for him, so I left him alone."

The news stunned Harley. Already her mind was swirling with the questions she would ask Brandon. When did you last see your sisters? Did they ever talk about leaving? Did you ever see anyone suspicious around the house? Did your sisters ever fear for their safety?

Stunted or not, Brandon could prove to be a gold mine of information. Harley sensed she might have just caught a huge break.

"I need to talk to him," she said, her excitement causing her to speak more quickly. "If his sisters were the killer's first victims, there's no telling what he might know."

The sheriff looked hesitant.

"What is it?" Harley said, hoping he wasn't about to burst her bubble.

"You can try talking to him, but chances are he won't say much. Brandon's not really the talkative type. I don't think he had much to say before his sisters disappeared, and the loss seems only to have driven him deeper inside his own head."

Harley thought of the dilapidated state of the farmhouse. Was its condition simply a manifestation of grief, of letting go? If so, the man needed an intervention.

"If I can get anything out of him," she answered, "it will be worth the trip. Does he have a job?"

Santiago shook his head. "He tried working down at Holy Hope – gathering eggs, cleaning potatoes, that kind of thing – but it didn't work out. He was too clumsy—did more harm than good much of the time."

"So how does he get by?"

"His sisters had a little money. It's not much, but you've seen how

143

he lives."

Harley recalled the greasy windows, the crumbling chimney. Brandon certainly didn't spend money on cleaning products and repairs.

"More than likely," the sheriff continued, "you'll find him at the farmhouse, puttering around. What he'll be doing, though—that's anyone's guess. I haven't crossed paths with him in months."

Harley nodded, excited to have something to go on. Maybe, just maybe, Brandon knew something that could help the investigation. The police would have taken a statement from him when his sisters went missing, but they would not have been looking for a serial killer. It was entirely possible they had glossed over details that could prove highly significant to Harley's case.

"Just be careful with him," the sheriff added.

Harley paused, uncertain what to make of Santiago's cautious tone. "Is he dangerous?"

"More like fragile. He doesn't get many visitors, and he seems to prefer it that way. Don't put him on the spot too much and you'll do fine."

She nodded. If she could handle sitting at a table across from John Kavers, she could handle talking with an emotionally stunted recluse.

"Thank you," she said as she started toward the door. "You have no idea how much help you've been."

The sheriff smiled. "I've always known you'd make a good investigator, ever since you were a teenager. Now go catch that son of a bitch before he kills again."

Harley smiled back, inspired by Santiago's confidence, and left the building. Her thoughts hummed with all the things she would ask Brandon.

As she pulled out of the lot, she realized she still hadn't talked with the sheriff about the voicemail he'd left. Maybe it was just as well. She would rather discuss it with him when they both had plenty of time to talk.

For now, she had a killer to catch.

144

CHAPTER TWENTY FIVE

Following the long ribbon of Sawyer Pass out to the farmhouse, Harley went through the details of the case in her head, trying to piece it all together. What troubled her most was the six-month gap. If the unsub – FBI-speak for "unknown subject" – had started with the two Rasco sisters, where had he been for the following six months? And why, all of a sudden, was he killing again?

The dark trees crowded the road. Harley slowed, not wishing to miss the turnoff, which was unmarked. In the darkness, everything outside the glow of the headlights was a ghostly gray, formless and unsteady as a mirage.

Keeping one hand on the wheel, Harley lifted her phone from the cupholder and dialed Callaway's number. She told herself she was doing this to keep her partner up-to-date, which was true, but it was equally true that she just wanted to hear the sound of a human voice.

She did hear a voice, but it was only the voicemail recording. Callaway had probably silenced his phone while he questioned Joseph Warren.

"This is Callaway. Leave a message."

Harley waited for the beep, slowing as she recognized the narrow path branching through the trees on her left.

"I'm heading over to the farmhouse on Sawyer Pass," she said into the phone as she turned. "The sisters had a brother, Brandon, who's still living here. I'm going to find out everything I can about the night his sisters went missing."

The headlights bobbed over the uneven path, hinting at the farmhouse as she neared it. No lights were on, and Harley could see no vehicles nearby.

"Call me back when you can," she continued, "and let me know if you make any progress on your end."

She hesitated, wanting to say something more but not sure what it was. She wondered if Callaway had learned anything new. Despite her doubts about Warren, she would have been more than happy to be proven wrong.

She turned off the headlights and took a few moments to let her eyes adjust to the darkness before getting out of the car. After locking the car, she approached the house. Something grunted off to her right—one of the pigs, she supposed.

A board creaked underfoot as she climbed the steps to the porch. She caught her foot on a nail that had worked itself up from the wood, and she nearly tripped, managing to prevent her fall by grabbing hold of the railing, which groaned with the effort of steadying her.

"Mr. Rasco?" she called. "Brandon Rasco?"

No answer came. She was beginning to wonder if Santiago had been mistaken. The sheriff hadn't seen Brandon in months, after all, so it was possible Brandon had moved on.

But the pigs, she thought. *They're skinny, yes, but they have to be eating* something *to stay alive.* Someone *is keeping an eye on them.*

Harley rapped the door with her knuckles. The hinges creaked as the door inched inward. She was certain it had been locked the night before, so apparently someone had been there since her last visit.

Turning on her flashlight, Harley nudged the door open the rest of the way, revealing a narrow hallway lined with dusty photographs, the plastered wall dark with dirt. The underlying odor of sweat and unwashed clothes, like a locker room, reached Harley's nostrils.

Stepping into the house, Harley paused to study the photographs. She had to brush the dust away to see them clearly. The first was a picture of the farmhouse under construction, a shirtless man – Rasco senior, Harley guessed – lining up his hammer with a nail he held pinched between the second and third fingers of his left hand, a second nail jutting from between his teeth. The second picture showed a small boy squatting in mud, his hands folded behind his back as he watched several piglets eating corn on the cob.

The third picture hung backwards, so that the photograph itself was hidden. Harley turned it around. The glass was cracked, but Harley could still make out a scene of three siblings posing for a picture, two girls flanking a boy. The girl on the right was a head taller than the boy, and the girl on the left was a head taller than the first one. They both wore floral-patterned dresses and had ribbons in their pigtails. The three were smiling as they held hands. They looked like a happy family.

Harley leaned closer. No, they were not exactly holding hands. The girls were holding the boy's wrists while his hands hung limp. And the girls' smiles—there was something overly cheerful about them, almost triumphant. The boy was smiling, too, but there was a haunted look to his eyes, as if they bore some terrible secret they could not forget.

Harley heard a rusty creak to her right and spun toward the sound,

146

startled. It was only the door shifting in the wind.

Unsettled by the darkness, Harley flipped the light switch at the base of the stairs. Nothing happened. Thinking the bulb might simply have gone out and never been replaced, she crossed the stairs and entered the room on the other side, a kitchen. Dishes were piled high in the sink, patterned with petrified food, and the trash can overflowed with plastic wrappers, fast food boxes, soda cans, and toilet paper cores. Thick spiderwebs spanned the space between the countertop to the backsplash, the heaps of bundled flies beneath them testifying further to the state of decay.

Again, Harley tried the lights, but nothing happened. She could hear the soft hum of the refrigerator, however, so there had to be power. Had Brandon – or whoever else had been here last – simply decided not to replace the lightbulbs?

Then, shining her flashlight up at the ceiling, she noticed the bulb was missing from the overhead light.

Odd, Harley thought.

She opened the refrigerator and was greeted by moldy cheese, curdled milk, and sliced ham gone slimy and pale with age. She covered her nose and closed the door, hoping she hadn't inhaled anything toxic.

The hoot of an owl startled her. She reached for her phone, overcome by a sudden urge to call for backup.

You're just being silly, she told herself. *What will you tell them, "I'm being attacked by a spooky old house"?*

Still covering her nose, she moved into the dining room. A dirty sleeping bag, torn in several paces, lay curled beneath the table like the shed skin of a snake.

She no longer had any doubt that someone had been living there. Given the state of the building, however, she wondered whether Santiago had really done Brandon any favors by leaving him alone. If this was how he lived, he needed assistance.

The air around Harley became dense and cloying. She needed open space, fresh air. Brandon was clearly not here at the moment, and Harley had no interest in hanging around until he returned. She would leave a card by the front door, then go on her merry way and wait for him to call her back.

Hurrying toward the front door, her flashlight panned across the hallway closet. She took a few more steps before realizing what she had seen.

It can't be, she thought as a chill coursed through her body.

Slowly turning back, as if she needed the time to prepare herself, she approached the closet and opened the door the rest of the way. Her heart hammered in her chest as she stooped to examine the pair of handmade sandals tucked at the back of the closet. Without touching them, she leaned into the closet so she could read the initials carved into the leather. They were faded, but still legible.

The initials were "E.R."

"Eleanor Renfrew," Harley whispered, covering her mouth.

CHAPTER TWENTY SIX

Maddie woke to the sensation of something crawling across her shoulder. It was too dark to see – even without the blindfold, she doubted she would have been able to see her hands in front of her face – but she could still feel things perfectly, and whatever was crawling across her skin was both large and furry.

Her first thought was that it was a tarantula. She had never been particularly scared of spiders, but something about waking to the feel of a spider crawling across her body felt...

Violating. Wrong.

Stifling a scream, she raised her hands to brush the critter away. The motion was difficult, since her hands were bound together with some kind of rough rope. It did not matter, however, because the creature crawled off and trundled away before she could reach it, its legs rasping across the floor.

Maddie breathed a sigh of relief. As she rested her head back down on the cold floor of packed earth, her mind turned to her present situation. She tried to piece together the events of the past twenty-four hours—a challenging exercise, since she didn't know how long she'd been sleeping.

She remembered helping Carol bring the horses into the barn. She had initially protested the idea – it was better for the horses to have space to roam, and she didn't see any reason to suspect someone would harm the horses, despite the recent killings – but when she saw how worried Carol was, she stopped arguing and decided to help.

Then...what? In heaven's name, what had happened next?

As the scene played out in her mind, she saw herself reaching into Bucky's stall to scratch his forehead. Then she ran her hand down to his nostrils, enjoying the softness of the skin. Her mind was somewhere else, going over the details of her last conversation with Warren as he gave her an ultimatum: respect the way he ran things, or get out of town. The choice was hers.

Then that awful moment when the rope was looped around her throat. She scratched at it with her fingernails as her attacker pulled her backward, leading her out through the open doors like a reluctant dog on a leash. She struggled, throwing back her elbow and eliciting a pained groan. But she knew it was a losing battle.

Her vision faded as her body took on a leaden weight.

Then she woke up here, in this dark vault smelling of mold and decay.

She hoped Carol was okay. If Carol was alive, she might be able to identify the killer. The only problem was, Maddie didn't know if she could wait that long. Her attacker – the same man, she had no doubt, who had killed four others in the community – might come back at any moment.

Back to do what? she thought. If he was planning to kill her, why hadn't he got it over with already? He could have killed her back at the barn, or in the truck. Unless, of course, he was keeping her alive because he didn't want to have to transport her dead weight. He might be cruising around right that moment, searching for a place to hide her body.

Don't think that way, she told herself. *You've gotten yourself out of plenty of situations before. You'll do the same thing again.*

Yes, she had. But it was one thing to deal with uncooperative clients, biased judges, and inept assistants, and it was quite a different thing to deal with a man intent on ending her life. No persuasive argument, no clever turn of phrase, was going to get her out of this situation.

Then I'll just have to jump him. He'll come down, and I'll grab him from behind just like he grabbed me. She moved her arms, imagining how she would slip the rope around his neck.

The only difference is, I won't stop squeezing, not until I'm sure he's out.

Could she really do it? She considered herself a tough person, but there were many kinds of toughness, not all of them physical. She hadn't been in a physical confrontation – not a truly hostile one – in all her life. Now she was supposed to choke a man out, knowing she could very well kill him if she held on too long?

Hoping she wouldn't have to find out what she was capable of, she rose on trembling legs and began moving about the room, one hand on the wall. Her fingers brushed a spiderweb and she recoiled with a shudder. As she stepped away, she stumbled over a crate and landed hard, bruising her shoulder. She cried out involuntarily.

Aware her attacker could still be nearby, she held her breath and listened for footsteps. She heard a creak overhead.

He's here! she thought as a wave of panic threatened to drive her under. *He's right above me!*

150

Then she heard a voice, distorted by distance and the floor so that it sounded mumbling, like a voice underwater. Still, there was something striking about the sound. It was decidedly…female.

Hope ran through her like an electric shock. She didn't know for certain whether her attacker was a man or a woman, but she felt certain, deep in her gut, that it had been a man, if only because the overwhelming majority of violent attacks were perpetrated by men.

"Help!" she tried to scream, but the gag muffled her words so that all that came out was a loud moan. She pushed at the gag with her tongue and managed to force it down, giving her a little more space.

"Help! He's going to kill me!"

She kicked at the wall, trying to make as much commotion as she could, but the stones made little sound. All she succeeded in doing was hurting her foot.

She fell silent, breathing heavily in the darkness. Waiting, listening.

Please don't leave, she prayed inwardly, *whoever you are. Please don't leave me here alone to wait for him.*

CHAPTER TWENTY SEVEN

Harley stood as still as a statue in the dark hallway, waiting to see whether the sound would come again.

Maybe you're just hearing things, she thought. *It is an old house, after all.*

But no, she felt certain she had heard a voice. Had it been Maddie's? Was she trapped somewhere nearby, waiting for rescue?

Harley looked again at the pair of sandals branded with Eleanor Renfrew's initials. It was something many killers did, bringing home mementos of their murders so they could relive the crime again and again in their fantasies. It didn't really matter what the object was so long as it brought the crime to life again, allowing the killer to savor the satisfaction of his dark deeds.

She thought of the sleeping bag tucked beneath the dining table, the moldy food in the refrigerator. Had this farmhouse served as the killer's hideout, his home base for perpetrating the murders? It made sense, given how close it was to Holy Hope.

All this time, she thought with a chill, *he's been right here.*

It was perhaps four or five miles to Holy Hope by road, but it would be much shorter in a straight line. The killer might have been approaching the community on foot—that would explain why Callaway hadn't heard him. Of course, it wouldn't explain how the killer had transported his victims.

She was still trying to puzzle it out when she heard that muffled sound again. This time it was unmistakable—yes, definitely a voice. Was it…grunting? Moaning? The sound seemed to be coming from another floor, though whether it was above or below her, she couldn't tell.

"Maddie!" she called. "Can you hear me?"

After waiting a few heartbeats and hearing nothing, she raced up the stairs to the second floor. She searched the rooms one after the other. The first was a storage room packed with old furniture, and after a quick peek around, Harley decided there was no way Maddie was in there. The second was an empty library—no place to hide a prisoner.

The third was a bedroom with two bunk beds made up with floral sheets. There was a dresser with a mirror, a pair of matching jewelry boxes, and a small closet. Harley opened the closet. It was narrow, perhaps two feet deep by six feet wide, with an old blanket on the floor and a torn pillow losing its feathers. Unintelligible markings had been scratched on the walls in looping, zig-zag patterns, like a child's drawings in the dark. A blunt nail lay in the corner.

And somehow, Harley knew this was the closet where Brandon's sisters had kept him shut up. How many nights had he slept there, scratching idly at the wall, alone in the darkness? How many of his screams had gone ignored?

She turned her flashlight to the back of the door. Deep gouges marred the wood. She could only imagine how frightened the boy must have been.

As disturbing as this discovery was, it did not get her any closer to finding Maddie, so she retraced her steps to the first floor. There had to be a basement. But she had already searched the first floor without finding a second set of stairs, so either there was a trap door hidden somewhere or the entrance was outside.

Not relishing the idea of crawling on hands and knees across the filthy floors, Harley hurried outside. She had to find Maddie before her kidnapper returned.

The front door gave an awful creak as it opened. Harley pulled out her phone and began calling Santiago as she crossed the porch. Just as she reached the steps, she noticed movement to her right. Before she could swing the flashlight toward it, however, something struck the side of her head and both the phone and the flashlight went flying from her hands. She felt herself sinking down, down, down into darkness.

*

When Harley opened her eyes again, she was lying on her side in the grass. The flashlight lay several feet away, pointing a cone of light at the side of the house. She must have fallen down the porch steps.

Not daring to move, she waited as her thoughts slowly gathered like metal filings drawn to a magnet. She wiggled her fingers and toes to make sure she still had use of them, but otherwise she gave no sign she was conscious because she knew she was not alone. She could hear someone's ragged breathing somewhere to her left, slowly getting closer.

Something prodded her back. It might have been a bony finger or a stick. She did not move, despite the discomfort.

"Beatrice," a low voice murmured in a teasing tone. "Oh, Beatrice.

I know you're awake. Don't play games with me."

Still Harley remained as she was. She could feel the Glock beneath her, pressing into her abdomen. She would have to roll onto her back to draw it. That would be a risky move, however, since she didn't know how far away her attacker was. Better to take her time and look for the right opportunity than risk escalating the action when she was at a disadvantage.

"I was beginning to think you might not come back," the voice purred. "But you surprised me, and what a wonderful surprise it is."

He was close, very close. Better to leave the gun where it was, then. But was he armed? He might still be carrying whatever he had struck her with.

"You're wondering where your sister is, aren't you?" he continued. "Don't worry, she's safe. She'll be very happy to see you, I'm sure."

Harley felt a finger trace the skin from her elbow on down to her wrist. The touch was light, almost sensual. Given the position of the thumb, she knew it had to be his left hand. He was probably either stooping over her or crouching behind her.

"You need to wake up, Beatrice," the voice cooed. "There is so much to do. You don't want to sleep the night away, do you?"

Every nerve in Harley's body was on high alert. She steeled herself, preparing to act. As his fingers began tracing her arm again, she reached out with her right hand and grabbed the man's thumb, wrenching it back. He cried out, recoiling, and she struck back with her left elbow. She felt the hard impact of bone. Then, releasing his hand, she rolled to her right and pushed herself to her feet.

An overpowering wave of dizziness rocked her, and she staggered a few steps, barely able to maintain her balance.

Come on! she urged herself desperately. *Focus!*

She heard a piteous moan from the darkness. As she tried to focus her eyes on the swirling yard, her vision suddenly clarified just in time for her to see her attacker hurtling toward her. He slammed into her waist, knocking her to the ground and winding her. She felt a sharp pain as the outline of a brick pressed into her back.

"Stupid little skink, stupid little skink!" the man hissed, maneuvering his knees so that he could pin her down. His hands were like vices on her wrists. A rank, sour odor bore over Harley.

Desperate to keep him from solidifying his hold on her, Harley bucked her hips and twisted her arms. He was thin but wiry, and he managed to keep his balance and stay on top of her.

"You're going to make me cross, Beatrice!" he hissed, leering down at her. The flashlight caught the edge of his face, revealing the dirty stubble of a mustache, pebbly dark eyes, and teeth brown as a cockroach.

Twisting her face away in disgust, Harley shifted sideways so that her left leg was between both of his. Then, with a sharp upward motion, she slammed her thigh into his groin. He shrieked, and she felt his grip on her wrists momentarily relax.

Taking advantage of his surprise, Harley sat up, grabbed his shirt with both hands, and shucked him to the side. As he fell, he grabbed at her gun, managing to pull it from the waistband of her jeans. It spilled into the grass, where he kicked at it before Harley could get her hands on it.

Harley, however, had received plenty of hand-to-hand training and did not need a firearm to subdue an attacker. She lunged toward him, planning to pin him to the ground in a hold until he gave up, but he rolled away just before she could reach him. He sprang lightly to his feet and stared at her, breathing raggedly as he drew a rusted knife from his belt.

"I'm not your sister," Harley said, brushing a lock of hair away from her face as she tried to reason with him. "But if you have Maddie, you need to tell me where she is. Do that, and this will all go a lot easier for you."

His face writhed with silent fury as if worms were crawling just beneath the skin. It was the impotent rage of someone who cannot take being bested—someone who, given the chance, would rather cheat than accept a fair loss.

She braced herself for him to come at her. Just when she thought he would snap and race toward her, however, he bolted, giving one hateful over-the-shoulder glance as he raced around the side of the house.

Spotting her Glock in the grass, Harley scooped it up. Then she gave chase, worried he would slip off into the woods and disappear in the darkness. It quickly became apparent he was not heading for the woods, however. Harley heard a metallic groan, and she reached the back of the house just in time to see Brandon Rasco descending through the open door of a bulkhead.

He's insane if he thinks I'm going to chase him down there, she thought, pulling up short. She wanted to call for backup, but her cell phone was somewhere in the grass of the front yard. Did she really dare risk him escaping while she went searching for it?

Her thoughts were interrupted by Rasco's voice calling to her from the bottom of the stairs, taunting her.

"Why don't you come down and see your sister? She's been so lonely down here without you—haven't you, Bella?"

"Please!" a female voice called up from the darkness. "He's dangerous!" Harley didn't recognize the voice, but she had to assume it belonged to Maddie Walsh.

"Go and get help!" Maddie said. "Run! Don't worry about me!"

There was a grunt, followed by a whimper. Then, one step at a time, two figures ascended the stairs. The killer had Maddie in a headlock, his knife pressed against her throat. The knife did not look very sharp, but the blood seeping from a pair of shallow cuts – created, Harley suspected, by the motion of climbing the stairs – showed it was sharp enough to do the job.

Harley aimed at Rasco's face. She didn't dare fire while he was so close to Maddie, but if he leaned away just a little, she might have a clear shot.

"Drop the gun," Rasco said. "Unless you want to wear dear Bella's blood."

"Don't hurt her," Harley said, her pulse pounding in her ears. "She hasn't done anything to you."

"Hasn't done anything? Have you forgotten *everything*?" He shook his head in disbelief. "All those nights I spent locked away? The times you made me sleep out with the pigs? You think I can just *forget* all of that like you can?"

The knife began to shake in his hands. The more agitated he became, the greater chance there was he would hurt Maddie, whether he intended to do so or not.

Rasco's voice dropped to a low, dangerous note. "You think I won't hurt her just because she's my sister?"

"No, I don't think that," Harley replied, her mind searching furiously for a way to defuse the situation. She needed time to think of a solution, but time was running out. She had no doubt the man was ready to sever Maddie's carotid, even if it meant Harley would gun him down.

"Then put...the gun...on the ground," he demanded through his teeth.

She was trapped. She licked her lips, desperately trying to think of a way out, but she couldn't think of anything. She needed to stall, to prevent Rasco from taking drastic action, and the only way to do that was to play along for now.

Careful not to make any sudden movements that might inspire Rasco to do something he couldn't take back, Harley stooped and set

156

the gun in the dirt.

"Now kick it away, hard as you can," the man ordered.

Harley did so, punting the pistol six or seven feet into the grass. She tried to mentally mark where it had gone, but she knew it would be difficult to find it a second time in the darkness.

The man's arms relaxed and he lowered the knife, smiling. "That's better, isn't it? Now turn around and start walking."

"Where are we going?" Harley said, dreading the answer.

"To the pen, of course." He giggled, delighted. "My piggies are hungry."

CHAPTER TWENTY EIGHT

As they moved toward the pig pen, Harley felt a flutter of panic in her gut. She realized now it had been a mistake to enter the farmhouse alone, even though she couldn't have known what was waiting for her. Callaway would come looking for her if he did not hear from her within a few hours, but did he even know how to reach the farmhouse? He could enlist Santiago's help, sure, but that would take more time.

Meanwhile, Harley and Maddie would be fighting for their lives.

Rasco could hide my Jeep in the woods, pretend he never saw me, she realized with a sinking feeling. Callaway would insist on looking around the house, sure, but would he think to check the pig pen?

If I don't think of something soon, my shoes might be the only thing left for Callaway to find.

Harley's gaze moved along the forest, searching for a means of escape. She noticed an old pickup with a dented bumper parked beneath a tree. She was certain it hadn't been there the previous night. Was that the vehicle Rasco had used to drop Sienna Davis's body off on the side of Coyote Creek Road? Had that dent been made by the impact of Eleanor Renfrew's body as Rasco ran her down?

"Keep up, Beatrice," Rasco chided. "We're going to do it right this time—do it right or do it twice, as Momma used to say."

Harley watched Rasco shuffle forward, half-dragging and half-pushing Maddie. Maddie's face was pale, and her eyes pleaded with Harley to do something. But what could Harley do?

"You don't have to do this," Harley began, her throat suddenly dry. "You can get help. There are medications, specialists for people in your situation."

"My situation," Rasco answered, sounding amused. "Now you want to help, do you, Beatrice? Well, you sure as hell didn't want to help before!" He gave Maddie a vicious jerk, the blade of the knife raking across her skin. Maddie whimpered helplessly.

As they neared the pig pen, it occurred to Harley there was no use arguing with Rasco's perception of reality. He believed he was reenacting the punishment of his two sisters, as he had no doubt been trying to do with every pair of women he attacked—a punishment that was, in his mind, a just response to the wrongful way he had been

158

treated for many years. Telling him he was wrong would only anger him further. Perhaps it would be better to play along and buy into his fantasy.

Mustering all the sympathy she could, Harley said, "I'm sorry for what we did to you, Bella and I. The way we…mistreated you." She trailed off. Why hadn't she dug more into his past, asked more questions of Santiago? She had been so short-sighted to come here unprepared.

Rasco slowed his pace, but he did not look at her. Nevertheless, she sensed she had his attention.

She had a flash of inspiration. "That's why you call yourself Skink, isn't it? We used to call you that."

"Dirty little skink," Rasco said in a teasing tone. "Why don't you go run and hide in some hole, you good-for-nothing little skink?"

"It must have been difficult, putting up with it all those years: the bullying, the name-calling. You were never good enough for us, were you?"

She saw Rasco's jaw work back and forth, but no words came out. She had heard the phrase "gnashing one's teeth" before, but she didn't think she had ever seen it in action until now. It was almost as if he were trying to chew a particularly tough piece of meat.

They were nearly at the fence. If she was going to convince him, she had to do so soon. She was running out of time.

"You're right to be angry about what happened to you," she continued, desperate for some way to break through to him. "It was wrong."

"And you need to be *punished*!" he answered with a vicious snarl.

"Yes, but you punished us already, didn't you? This already happened. Do you remember it, Rasco?"

He was silent.

They had reached the fence. Harley could see tiny pinpricks of light coming from the shed toward the back of the enclosure. The pigs' eyes, gleaming in the starlight.

Rasco gestured with the knife at the fence. "Climb in."

Harley shook her head. "I can't do that, Brandon."

"Then your sister dies!" he shouted, spit flying from his mouth as he pressed the knife more firmly against Maddie's throat. She swallowed, and the motion of her throat against the knife drew a fresh line of blood.

"It's going to be okay, Maddie," Harley said, staring into the woman's eyes, hoping Maddie couldn't see the desperate uncertainty

Harley felt. "Everything is going to be alright."

"Get in the pen!" Rasco shouted.

With no other way out, Harley began to climb the fence boards. Her hands shook, and her mind raced as she tried to come up with some scenario in which she and Maddie both survived the night. She could only hope the pigs, hungry as they were, would know the difference between predator and prey. If she could convince them she was more dangerous than they were, if she could keep them from getting riled up, it might give her time to think of another solution.

Then Rasco reached for the dinner bell. He shook it violently, his mouth grinning so wide that it looked like it might split his face. "Time to eat, little piggies!" he cried, nearly jumping up and down in his excitement. "Time for dinner!"

A gaggle of squeaks and squeals issued from the darkness. Shapes raced toward Harley like a swarm of bats, crawling over one another in their haste.

Her heart in her throat, Harley clambered up the fence. The board cracked, threatening to break entirely.

"No!" Rasco shrieked. The knife in his hand had gone slack as he watched the pigs rush at Harley, but now the tip stabbed against Maddie's throat. "Get back in or she dies!"

Seeing the wildness in Rasco's eyes, Harley had no doubt he was moments away from slicing Maddie's throat open. She could either throw herself to the pigs or let Maddie bleed out.

The pigs began to nip at Harley's shoes, tugging at her, grasping the laces in their little teeth. One caught the cuff of her pants, and she felt something hard and sharp drag along the back of her ankle as the pig pulled at her pants.

All she had to do was let go of the fence and fall back. How long would it take? Would they go for her throat, or would they start with whatever was closest: a hand, a foot, an ear, a nose? The very thought was unbearable...and yet, somehow, it was less unbearable than the sight of Maddie's eyes pleading with her to do something, to find a way to make everything right.

I can't this time, Harley thought, looking at the feverish gleam in Rasco's eyes. *I can't reason with him, I can't trick him, I can't overpower him.* She could only hope that when she threw herself into the pen, the distraction would give Maddie an opening, a chance to get away.

If that was all Harley's death accomplished, it would be worth the sacrifice.

160

One of her shoelaces tore free. A snout went snuffling up her leg, nipping at the flesh beneath the fabric.

Harley's hands relaxed on the fence. She leaned back and closed her eyes, praying that somehow Maddie would find a way to escape.

Just as she was letting go of the fence, a light swept across her closed eyelids like a searchlight. She opened her eyes to see Rasco twisted toward the headlights of an approaching vehicle, the hand with the knife raised to shield his eyes. A surge of desperate hope welled up in Harley.

Taking advantage of the distraction, Maddie drove her elbow into Rasco's ribs and slipped from his grasp. As Maddie moved aside, Harley launched herself from the top of the fence, slamming into Rasco and knocking him to the ground. He rolled away and sat up, an expression of groggy confusion on his face.

The blade of the knife was stuck fast in the ground between them, the hilt protruding. For a split second they both stared at it, their shocked minds lagging just a moment behind. Then, as if on cue, they both scrambled toward it, crawling on all fours like dogs.

Rasco reached the knife first. He ripped it from the dirt and straightened, smiling triumphantly.

The glare of the headlights, however, was in his eyes. As he squinted, searching for Harley, she rushed close and kicked him in the chest. His arms pinwheeled as he staggered backward, striking the fence where Harley had cracked it. The board broke, and Rasco fell into the pen, his head and shoulders sinking into mud. There was an excited squeal as the pigs descended on him.

"Help!" he screamed, flailing as he tried to use the fence to pull himself up. One of the boards pulled free, and he fell back.

The pigs crowded around him, snuffling and nipping at his limbs, his fingers, his hair. One of the pigs tore off part of his ear, and he screamed, writhing like a beetle turned on its back. For a moment Harley felt no pity, not for such a ruthless killer as this one. What pity had he shown his victims? What pity had he shown her?

Don't be like him, she told herself. *Don't stoop to his level.*

Springing into action, she grabbed one of his ankles and dragged him toward herself. She reached down through the cluster of greedy mouths and caught his hand.

Harley found herself in a tug-of-war with the pigs, Brandon Rasco caught between them. Then, planting her feet, she gave a hard pull and felt Rasco come free. She staggered back, catching her balance, ready to subdue Rasco should he try to rise. But he just lay on the ground, panting and murmuring to himself.

Harley leaned on her legs, her whole body shaking as relief washed over her. One of the pigs screeched and she shuddered, imagining the fate she had almost just suffered.

A car door clapped shut nearby.

"FBI!" Callaway shouted as he rushed over, gun drawn. He stopped abruptly, looking from Harley, to the pigs, to Rasco, to Maddie, then finally to Harley again. He didn't seem to know what to make of what he was seeing.

He turned to Maddie, whose chest heaved with sobs. "Are you Maddie Walsh?" he said.

She nodded, unable to speak. Tears streamed down her face.

"You're safe now," Harley assured her. "You're okay. He's not going to harm you."

Leaving Maddie with Harley, Callaway knelt on Rasco's back and cuffed his hands. The sound of his voice reading Rasco his rights droned on in the background while Harley rubbed Maddie's back.

"Are you hurt?" she said, trying to see how bad the cuts on Maddie's throat were. It was difficult to tell in the poor light.

Maddie shook her head and sniffed hard. "Not badly. What about Carol? Is she alright?"

"She's fine. Has a good bruise on the back of her head, but that's about it. She's recovering at the hospital now."

Maddie nodded as another sob burst from her chest. Harley put her arms around her and held her, as much for her own comfort as for Maddie's. One of the pigs grunted, and it occurred to Harley they might find a way out through the broken fence. She would have to call a local shelter. It was high time they were taken care of.

"Come on," Callaway said, pulling Rasco to his feet. "I think you've had enough fun for one night." He marched Rasco to the truck. Rasco kept his head lowered, one hand to his bloody ear, muttering to himself. He would be a victim to the very end, Harley suspected.

After securing Rasco, Callaway returned to Harley and Maddie.

"Can I have a word?" he said to Harley.

They stepped away.

"What the hell were you thinking, running off like that?" he hissed. "You could've gotten yourself killed! If I had stayed to talk with Warren a little longer, if I hadn't assumed the worst..." He shook his head, as if unable to countenance the thought of what might have happened.

Harley sensed that beneath all Callaway's anger was the fear he

162

could have lost her. Losing a partner was one of the worst things that could happen to an agent. He would have felt responsible, and he would have no doubt carried that guilt with him for the rest of his life, warranted or not.

Overwhelmed by everything that had happened, Harley stepped forward and threw her arms around Callaway. She glimpsed the way his eyebrows rose in surprise. Then, after a moment, he hugged her back.

"Thank you for coming," she whispered, hardly trusting her voice. She wanted to cry, but she knew that if she began now, there was no telling when it would stop.

Callaway's hand moved up and down her back—tentatively at first, then with greater confidence. After a few moments, Harley pulled away and knuckled her eyes.

The wail of an approaching siren grew louder in the distance, rolling across the dark and wooded hills, waking the night. Harley glanced at the silhouette of Rasco, rocking slowly back and forth in the back of Callaway's truck. She wondered if any part of him felt relieved at coming out of the shadows, if there was any innocence left in him at all, a small spark that had not been smothered by the daily torment of his sisters.

She wanted to believe there was, because then maybe there weren't any monsters after all, just regular people who had lost themselves in a maze of bad choices. Maybe, with enough time, even the worst of hurts could be healed.

"I can't believe it's all over," Maddie murmured. Her tears had dried, and there was a look of weary disbelief on her face. Harley knew that look well. It would take a long time for Maddie to process what had happened since being attacked in that barn. Harley, too, would live with the knowledge that if Callaway had arrived a mere five minutes later, she might very well have been beyond saving.

Callaway waved the ambulance forward. One of the paramedics stepped down and began asking Maddie questions, while a police car pulled up and a pair of officers climbed out. Callaway directed the officers to Rasco—it would be far safer to transport him in the back of a squad car than in Callaway's truck, which was not designed to contain criminals.

A sense of unreality washed over Harley as she watched all this transpire.

"Are you alright?" Callaway said as the paramedic began cleaning the cuts on Maddie's neck.

Harley considered the question. "I was just seconds away from being fed to a herd of feral pigs, so no, I'm not alright."

Callaway watched her, a solemn frown on his face.

Harley met Maddie's eyes for a moment. Maddie gave her a small nod, as if to say the worst of the storm had passed and she was still standing, her roots intact.

"I'm not alright," Harley continued, taking courage from Maddie's gaze, "but I will be. I will be."

Callaway touched her arm and leaned close to her face, close enough that she could see the crow's feet gathered at the corners of his eyes. "Good. Because I'm not ready to give up my new partner."

CHAPTER TWENTY NINE

Harley was stirring the olive in her martini when she heard a long sigh to her left. She turned as Callaway sat down next to her at the bar of the Feathered Finch, straightening his jacket as he did so.

"This seat taken?" he said, setting his hat on the bar and combing his hair with his fingers.

"It is now," Harley replied.

A few days had passed since the close of the investigation, long enough for Harley to catch up on some much-needed sleep and settle into her new home. Newbury had wanted her to take the week off, but she had convinced him she would go crazy without any work to do for an entire week, so they had settled on two days. Tomorrow she would report to the Santa Fe field office. As good as it would feel to get back into the swing of things, she secretly hoped she might have a few slow weeks before the next major case.

Callaway ordered a stout. When it arrived, he took a tentative sip and then set it back down.

"I was never much of a drinker," he said. He cast Harley a sidelong glance. "I can hold my own, mind you, but it never seemed much of a solution for me, getting drunk. It's like shooting yourself in the foot to solve a toothache."

Harley smiled, still stirring her martini. She sensed he was looking for closure, a way to put the case behind him so he could move on to the next one—which was often easier said than done. At least they knew the killer was behind bars. The cases that went unsolved were usually the ones that kept an agent up at night.

"I really thought Warren was our guy," Callaway mused as a cheer erupted behind them over a goal scored in the televised soccer game. "I guess I *wanted* it to be him because he deserved to be locked away."

"He'll get time," Harley assured him. "That statutory rape charge is solid."

After the allegations had surfaced, Violet and a few of the other teenage girls had come forward with stories about Warren touching them and trying to lure them into his house. A few of Warren's neighbors also testified to seeing Isla entering his home late at night and leaving early in the morning. Most damning of all, however, was the revelation that Joseph Warren had once been Walter Gallet, a priest at a Catholic school in southern Florida who had been defrocked after numerous complaints about "inappropriate interactions" with the students, not all of them female. He had been moved around to a few different schools before the allegations became too much of an embarrassment and he was removed from office.

"Besides, I doubt the judge will look kindly on his attempt to reenact the Jonestown Massacre," Harley added, referring to the plans discovered in Warren's house to lead the entire community in a mass suicide. That was probably why Warren had been at Maddie's house the night of her disappearance: to convince her to join his plan. It was also, Harley suspected, why he had behaved in such a nonchalant way throughout the interrogation process. What did a man planning to end his own life have to fear from the FBI?

Callaway nodded, gazing thoughtfully at the amber foam of his beer which hid the dark depths beneath. "You did good work, you know," he said. Then he straightened and looked Harley dead in the eye, as if to make sure she knew he was sincere.

She looked away, uncomfortable with such a straightforward compliment. "It was a team effort."

"This isn't a press release. I know it was a team effort, but if you hadn't come across that farmhouse…" He trailed off, spreading his hands and lifting his eyebrows. Harley knew what he was implying. If she hadn't found the farmhouse, there was no telling how many more bodies there would be.

"I'm not saying you handled it well," Callaway added. "You almost got yourself killed right along with Ms. Walsh."

"Is this where I thank you for saving my life?"

He shrugged modestly.

"Thank you for saving my life," she said to humor him. Then she touched his arm and said in a softer voice, "Seriously, those pigs would be polishing off my bones right now if not for you. And without Maddie taking over the leadership at Holy Hope and providing some much-needed common sense, there's no telling what would happen to them."

It was Callaway's turn to look uncomfortable. He took a long swallow of beer and cleared his throat.

A thoughtful silence settled between them. Harley sipped her martini as a waitress passed behind her and the scent of nachos wafted across the bar. Harley's mind drifted to her house: where she would set up the remaining pieces of furniture, whether there was any point paying for cable if she would be gone most of the time, when she would update the appliances.

"You ever think about the type of people we hunt?" Callaway said.

Harley answered automatically. "All the time. I'm a profiler."

"What they have in common, I mean. They're all victims in their own way, aren't they?"

This philosophical turn surprised Harley. She glanced at his beer, thinking he hadn't had nearly enough for the alcohol to start doing the talking.

"It's like the saying, 'Hurt people hurt people,'" he continued. "Show me someone who victimizes the vulnerable, and I'll show you someone who was victimized when he was vulnerable. It's this cycle, and we're all just passing on the terrible things that have been done to us."

"It doesn't have to be that way."

"No? How do you break out? Because it seems to me that once it becomes a habit, you're trapped. That's why serials go on killing till they're caught. They don't have a change of heart, suddenly give up killing because of a crisis of conscience. If they did, they'd confess to their crimes."

"Some do," Harley pointed out.

"It's the exception, by far."

"Maybe they just need a chance to start fresh with a clean slate."

"Like they were doing at Holy Hope?"

Harley considered this. "With the right leaders in place, it might have worked out. It still might, now that Maddie's taking an active part in things."

They both fell silent.

"One thing I still don't get," Callaway said. "Why was Eleanor wearing those sneakers?"

Harley herself had puzzled over this for a while. "They were Beatrice's," she answered.

Callaway's gaze was blank.

"The older sister," she explained. "When Rasco fed his sisters to the pigs, he didn't realize the pigs wouldn't eat their shoes. So later on, before the police showed up to investigate the missing persons' report filed by their mother when she couldn't reach them to ask for money, he found the muddy shoes and put them back in the house. The police probably didn't think anything of them."

"I get all that," Callaway answered. "But how'd they end up on Eleanor's feet?"

Harley pushed her martini aside and swiveled her stool so that she was facing Callaway. "He was reenacting the murder of his sisters, right? That's why he killed two women at a time. When he found Sienna and Eleanor along the road after Jacob Boudoin had dropped them off, he probably made Eleanor put on the shoes. It was his way of visualizing the crime better, making it more like the real thing."

"I don't understand why she didn't just ditch them. Must have been uncomfortable, running in those shoes all the way from Sawyer Pass to Lovers' Lane."

Harley had pondered this already. "Lots of cacti in that area. I'd rather deal with uncomfortable shoes than get a cactus spine through my foot, wouldn't you?"

Callaway shrugged. "I suppose. I wonder what she was thinking, crossing the road in front of him like that. Maybe she stepped out, thinking he was a good Samaritan coming to help. Then, by the time she realized who it was, there was no time to get away."

Before Harley could reply, her phone vibrated on the bar. She glanced down to see a message from her father.

Out of hospital. Have something for u. Where to meet

"Your new boyfriend?" Callaway guessed.

"My father. And I already told you, Bryce isn't my boyfriend." Bryce was stopping by that evening to celebrate the successful conclusion of the case with her, but Callaway didn't need to know that. She didn't want to have to put up with his snide remarks, at least not until she had a clearer idea of Bryce's intentions.

Callaway held up his hands, feigning innocence.

Curious as to what her father might want to give her, Harley texted back her address. *Stop by any time,* she added. *I'll be home the rest of the evening.*

"How's he doing?" Callaway said in a more serious tone.

"We're not sure how much time he has left. Could be a few days, a few weeks. A lot of it depends on how much he wants to stay alive."

Callaway nodded, pressing his lips together sympathetically.

Harley finished her martini. When she pulled out her wallet, however, Callaway covered it with his hand. "I've got this," he said.

"Next one's on me, then," she answered. "See you tomorrow?"

He raised his beer to her. "Bright and early."

She nodded, feeling reassured by the knowledge that she didn't have to worry about catching a flight back east, didn't have to wonder how long it would be before she returned. This was her life now, her world. This was where she belonged.

"May I make a suggestion?" Callaway said as she started to move away.

"What's that?"

"Next time, when you're thinking of searching a dark house for a serial killer, call for backup—preferably *before* you go in."

She raised an eyebrow. "Worried about me, Agent Callaway?"

He smiled. "I've learned there's no point worrying about you, Harley Cole. You're going to do things your own damn way, no matter what I think. There's no sense in me getting an ulcer over something I can't fix."

She laughed softly. "See you tomorrow, Callaway."

"See you tomorrow, Cole."

As she crossed the bar and stepped out into the warm night air, she realized she had made the right choice coming back. This was, and always would be, her home.

EPILOGUE

Harley was reaching for the knob of her front door when it swung open and she saw Bryce smiling at her, a hand towel thrown over his shoulder. A savory smell wafted from the house—something with curry, she suspected.

"Can I help you with something, ma'am?" he said, playfully raising an eyebrow.

Harley was surprised—she hadn't expected him to arrive for another twenty minutes. She had told him he could let himself in, if necessary, but she'd expected to get there before he did.

He's up to something, she thought. And she found she did not mind at all.

"I need a solid meal and a long, peaceful sleep," she answered, playing along. "Know anywhere I can find those?"

Bryce stepped aside and gestured for her to enter. "You've come to the right place. *Bienvenue, mademoiselle.*"

Harley stepped inside the house, following a row of candles nestled in Mason jars along the countertop. As she entered the dining room, she discovered two more candles on the dining table, which had been covered with a red tablecloth and set for two.

Harley took a sharp breath, stunned by his thoughtfulness. "Bryce, you didn't have to do all this!" When he had asked about stopping by, she'd thought they would go out to dinner—nothing fancy, just a chance to catch up. This was far more than she'd expected.

He leaned against the wall and grinned at her, his eyes dancing merrily in the firelight. "I figured you needed a chance to relax, unwind a little. Now pull up a chair while I take out our dinner. It's been staying warm in the oven."

To Harley's surprise, she discovered she had no interest in arguing. She pulled out one of the chairs and dropped into it. She took her phone from her pocket, put it on silent mode, and set it in the chair beside her. She could stop by her dad's place tomorrow. Whatever he wanted to talk about, it would probably be better to have the conversation when they were both rested.

"I wish I could say I cooked it myself," Bryce said as he emerged from the kitchen with a glass dish clutched between his mitten-covered hands, "but cooking's not my strong suit. If you need help birthing a calf, on the other hand…"

He set the dish down, then returned to grab a few more dishes. There was chicken tikka masala, biryani, a plate of samosas, lamb kebab, and other foods Harley could not name.

"This smells and looks *amazing*," she said, swallowing compulsively as her mouth filled with saliva. "Where'd you get it?"

Bryce shrugged modestly. "I know a place."

"Memories of the East?"

He shook his head. "They closed years ago. This is from Spice of Life."

"Never heard of that one. I guess I'll have to update my knowledge of the area, figure out what's still around and what isn't."

"I'm more than happy to help."

She smiled, pleased by the idea but not wanting them to get ahead of themselves. "For now, I'll settle for you passing me a samosa."

Harley had just finished making her first plate when there was a knock at the door. She groaned, frustrated by the timing.

Bryce rose, but Harley put a hand on his wrist to stop him. "No, I'll get it. It's my new home, after all. Just please, try not to eat *everything* before I get back?"

He grinned. "You'd better be quick, then."

Harley walked to the door, smiling and shaking her head. She was still smiling as she opened the door and saw her father standing in the entryway, a folder tucked beneath his arm. He was dressed in slacks and a sweater that looked far too thick for such a warm night. The clothing seemed to hang off him, as if several sizes too large, and there was an unhealthy pallor to his face as he gazed at her, unsmiling.

"You hate surprises, I know," he said, looking down as if he had crossed a line by showing up at her house. "But I was hoping you'd make an exception."

She hesitated, unsure whether to invite him in. She started to do so, turning so that he could pass her, but he made a quick shake of his head.

"I don't want to intrude," he said. "I know you have company." He paused, and the silence hung thick between them. She was relieved to hear water running in the bathroom, which suggested Bryce probably couldn't hear their conversation.

"I debated whether or not to do this," he began, his eyes roving across the floor as if he might find the words in the carpet. "When you lived so far away, it seemed irrelevant. But now that you're back…"

He sighed and pulled the folder out.

"What's this?" Harley said, feeling a stirring of unease but unsure why.

"Everything I've learned, going back to the beginning—notes, interviews, theories, all of it. I gave it the best I could, but I'm too old for this kind of thing. Besides, maybe you'll find something I missed."

His words gave her chills, and it took a few moments for her to understand the meaning of his words. "You kept a file on Kelly's disappearance all these years?" she replied, unable to believe he had hidden this from her for so long.

"I had to. Don't be angry with me for not sharing it sooner, okay? I didn't want it to just be a...a distraction for you. You couldn't juggle your job and your marriage on top of flying out here to investigate ancient history. But now that you're in the area..."

But she wasn't angry. She was grateful, and she felt a touch of admiration that her father hadn't given up when the investigators did.

"Is that why Sheriff Santiago called me?" she said. "He told me there had been a 'development' on Kelly's case, but he didn't say what it was."

"He thought you should know what I'd been working on, so that was his way of forcing my hand." He laughed ruefully. "If I didn't tell you, he would. But that's all moot now that you're here. My plan was always to tell you, if you ever moved back."

"Thanks, Dad," she murmured, taking the file. "All this time, I thought you had just given up. But you didn't. You held on."

She felt a newfound respect for her father. As much as she would have liked to know this sooner, she knew he had been right to wait. She wouldn't have been able to hold onto her marriage and her job while trying to solve her sister's disappearance at the same time, and if this file had been the reason for her divorce, her father would have felt responsible.

He nodded stiffly. "It's in your hands now. If anyone's ever going to figure out what happened to Kelly...it'll be you."

He cleared his throat, as if unsure what to do next. Then, without another word, he turned around. He had only taken a few steps when Harley's words stopped him.

"You said, 'If only she had listened to me the first time.' What did you mean?"

Her father gave her the ghost of a smile. "Read the file, Harley. It's all in there."

She watched her father make his slow way back to his car, his

172

shoulders bent forward slightly as if bracing himself against a stiff wind. The cape of invincibility he had once worn was long gone, and it occurred to Harley that she could no longer depend on her father to look out for her. *She* had to look out for *him*.

He didn't even turn his head around as he backed down the driveway, just watched the mirrors as the vehicle rolled back. He stopped in the road, shifted into drive, and glanced at Harley. Harley could barely see his face, but she felt certain he was smiling that sad, world-weary smile of his.

"Everything alright?" Bryce said, touching her shoulder.

Her gaze lingered on the taillights of her father's car shrinking into the night. "Yeah, it was just my dad stopping by."

"How is the old man? I haven't seen him in years."

"Not bad, all things considered. Stage Four lung cancer."

The humor fell from Bryce's face. "Harley, if I'd known—"

She shook her head, dismissing the apology. "I don't want to talk about it. Let's just enjoy tonight, okay? I don't want to ruin this."

He smiled and offered his hand. She closed the door and let him draw her deeper into this new house that was becoming a little bit more her home with every passing hour. On the way to the table, she slipped the file beneath the pile of mail on the counter.

"What's that?" Bryce said.

"Just some information about an old case," she answered. "It's probably nothing."

He nodded. "Sometimes it's hard to tell where work ends and life begins, isn't it?"

She said nothing as he carried their plates to the kitchen so he could heat them back up. She felt disconnected from reality, as if her world had been turned upside down. All these years, her father had been compiling notes on Kelly's disappearance. All the times he'd urged her to let go of the past, he'd failed to take his own advice.

The microwave began to hum. Bryce's fingers beat a jig on the counter as he waited.

"I'm just going to run to the bathroom," Harley said.

"Don't be long!" he called back. "We keep reheating this food; it's going to taste like cardboard."

Harley knew she would not be long. All she needed was five minutes, no more. Just five minutes.

As she passed the counter, she scooped up the file and carried it with her to the bathroom.

She had some catching up to do.

NOWHERE TO RUN
(A Harley Cole FBI Suspense Thriller—Book 3)

"This is an excellent book... When you start reading, be sure you don't have to wake up early!"
—Reader review for The Killing Game

When a teen tour heading downriver discovers a body, it is soon apparent this is the work of a new killer. FBI special agent Harley Cole, in a race against time, is assigned to navigate the tough terrain and stop this killer—but the demons of her past have finally caught up, and this time, there is no escape.

Nowhere to Run (A Harley Cole FBI Suspense Thriller—Book 3) is the third book in a new series by #1 bestselling mystery and suspense author Kate Bold, that begins with Nowhere Safe (book #1).

A page-turning and harrowing crime thriller featuring a brilliant and tortured FBI agent, the HARLEY COLE series is a riveting mystery, packed with non-stop action, suspense, twists and turns, revelations, and driven by a breakneck pace that will keep you flipping pages late into the night. Fans of Rachel Caine, Teresa Driscoll, and Robert Dugoni are sure to fall in love.

Future books in the series will soon be available.

"This book moved very fast and every page was exciting. Plenty of dialogue, you absolutely love the characters, and you were rooting for the good guy throughout the whole story... I look forward to reading the next in the series."
—Reader review for The Killing Game

"Kate did an amazing job on this book and I was hooked from the first chapter!"
—Reader review for The Killing Game

"I really enjoyed this book. The characters were authentic, and I see the bad guys as something we hear about daily on the news... Looking forward to book 2."
—Reader review for The Killing Game

"This was a really good book. The main characters were real, flawed and human. The story went along quickly and wasn't mired in too many unnecessary details. I really enjoyed it."
—Reader review for The Killing Game

"Alexa Chase is headstrong, impatient, but most of all brave with a capital B. She never, repeat never, backs down until the bad guys are put where they belong. Clearly five stars!"
—Reader review for The Killing Game

"Captivating and riveting serial murder with a twist of the macabre... Very well done."
—Reader review for The Killing Game

"WOW what a great read! Talk about a diabolical killer! Really enjoyed this book. Looking forward to reading others by this author as well."
—Reader review for The Killing Game

"Page turner for sure. Great characters and relationships. I got into the middle of this story and couldn't put it down. Looking forward to more from Kate Bold."
—Reader review for The Killing Game

"Hard to put down. It has an excellent plot and has the right amount of suspense. I really enjoyed this book."
—Reader review for The Killing Game

"Extremely well written, and well worth buying and reading. I can't wait to read book two!"
—Reader review for The Killing Game

Kate Bold

Bestselling author Kate Bold is author of the ALEXA CHASE SUSPENSE THRILLER series, comprising six books (and counting); the ASHLEY HOPE SUSPENSE THRILLER series, comprising six books (and counting); the CAMILLE GRACE FBI SUSPENSE THRILLER series, comprising five books (and counting); and the HARLEY COLE FBI SUSPENSE THRILLER series, comprising three books (and counting).

An avid reader and lifelong fan of the mystery and thriller genres, Kate loves to hear from you, so please feel free to visit www.kateboldauthor.com to learn more and stay in touch.

BOOKS BY KATE BOLD

ALEXA CHASE SUSPENSE THRILLER
THE KILLING GAME (Book #1)
THE KILLING TIDE (Book #2)
THE KILLING HOUR (Book #3)
THE KILLING POINT (Book #4)
THE KILLING FOG (Book #5)
THE KILLING PLACE (Book #6)

ASHLEY HOPE SUSPENSE THRILLER
LET ME GO (Book #1)
LET ME OUT (Book #2)
LET ME LIVE (Book #3)
LET ME BREATHE (Book #4)
LET ME FORGET (Book #5)
LET ME ESCAPE (Book #6)

CAMILLE GRACE FBI SUSPENSE THRILLER
NOT ME (Book #1)
NOT NOW (Book #2)
NOT WELL (Book #3)
NOT HER (Book #4)
NOT NORMAL (Book #5)

HARLEY COLE FBI SUSPENSE THRILLER
NOWHERE SAFE (Book #1)
NOWHERE LEFT (Book #2)
NOWHERE TO RUN (Book #3)

Made in the USA
Monee, IL
10 January 2023

25077202R00106